BIRTHDAY HOROSCOPES

CHARACTER READINGS

BY

DR. J. R. PHELPS

"The wise man rules his stars.
The fool obeys them."

WILDSIDE PRESS

FOREWORD

IT is a well known fact that many of our outstanding leaders in industry and finance consult reputable astrologers before embarking upon important undertakings. Internationally famous seers, such as Evangeline Adams, broadcasting over the radio, have acquainted millions of listeners with some of the rudiments of what is being recognized as the science of astrology. There is a growing popular interest in the study of the planetary influences upon our actions and destinies, and a decided need for a straightforward book of horoscope readings based upon the aspect of the heavens at the time of our nativity.

Whether you accept this work seriously as a volume of character readings based on science, a guide to happiness and success, or as a book wherewith to entertain a gathering of your friends; the author will have the satisfaction of knowing that he has contributed in some small part to one of the most interesting and useful of the human sciences.

INTRODUCTION

We commence our year with the sign Aries, as Aries is the beginning—the *sunrise* of the year, and stands also as the head of the "Grand Man," which the gifted seer Swedenborg teaches is the astrological form of the universal heavens.

Another feature of this book is seen in the division of the signs into sections. Leaving planetary influences out of the question—and the limits of our space will not allow us more than thus simply to allude to this potent factor in one's nativity—the various *degrees* of the same sign differ in their characteristics. Therefore every person born under Scorpio will not exhibit characteristics similar to those of every other person born under the same sign. There will certainly be a *basic* similarity of *nature,* but the *expressions* will be varied. Why this variation in the different degrees of the same sign exists, or its nature, would take too long to explain, so we simply state its existence as a fact.

And it is well to here note an important point. In human creation in the "cusp people," or those born with the sun on the dividing line of two signs, the nature partakes of the characteristics of both signs, although the influence of the sign out from which the sun is passing is generally supposed to be most potent. When the sun has progressed five degrees into a sign, the influence of the preceding sign is generally supposed to have come to an end.

The vastness of the subject of astrology renders it easy to be—in fact, almost impossible *not* to be—prolix in verbiage. One cannot skim over the surface of this science and *learn* much of it. He finds himself,—as in every other questioning of the forces that play upon our wonderful human life,—constantly confronted with mysteries that can be explained only by other mysteries, until he is convinced that Emerson strikes the truth when he writes:

> "Profounder, profounder, man's spirit must dive;
> His aye-rolling orbit at no goal will arrive;
> The heavens that now draw him with sweetness untold,
> Once found—for *new* heavens he spurneth the old."

Although astrology—like every other science—is an *"exact science,"* our conception and comprehension of it is far from exact. In the words of an esteemed friend, "Human science, gauged by our knowledge, is the lamest duck in the universe." Astrology is no exception to this truth. Astrological science is a dissected map of which many fragments are lost—to us of this earth. The course of a river as indicated on the portions that we have arranged give assurance that it flows *across* the missing section, but with what sinuosities and meanderings we may not as yet know. And so, as with *all* sciences, our conceptions—or knowledge, if you prefer the word—must, for some time to come, rest on—pardon the term—*empiricism.*

THE AUTHOR.

Index to Readings

NOTICE.—To find your birthday reading locate the month, and opposite the date of your birth is the page. The entire reading of a sign applies in general to all persons born within the sign under the groups of dates, though there are special features under each group or separate date, indicating special points for those of that date.

BIRTHDAY HOROSCOPES

Our Astrological Readings

Sign of Zodiac ARIES

Begins March 22—Ends April 20

GEM: AMETHYST. COLORS: YELLOW AND RED.

March 22, 23, 24, 25, 26.

Occupations: Judge, Lawyer, Teacher, Merchant, Financier, Business Manager.

Born on the cusp of Pisces and Aries, your nature partakes of the characteristics of both signs. You have the faculty of projecting business enterprises, and the capacity for carrying them out. You are enthusiastic and kind, and, if an employer, you will be able to inspire your employees—or those of them who are capable of being inspired—with good measure of your own vigor and determination. If you are an employee, you are faithful, equally enthusiastic, but must do everything according to your own methods. Any material interference in your details will disarrange them, and be apt to awaken an unexplainable and uncontrollable obstinacy that may result in your throwing up the whole business. If you are a woman, you will be fond of having many admirers, but will not be strongly drawn towards marriage, unless the man who seeks to win you masters your affections and desires by his own worthiness, and then he becomes your god. If you are a man, you will be apt to be drawn more strongly towards marriage, but very apt to "spy out the land" before settling down. Although very warm-hearted, you are not a creature of impulse. You stop to see what is to be made by any serious move, but are generous in sharing your happiness with those you love.

You start out in an undertaking, after you have decided to start, at full speed. If mentally excitable through planetary influences, you can—probably will—be domineering, perhaps not necessarily in an offensive way.

Special to March 24, 25, 26.

You have an inflexible love of justice, especially in what is due to yourself, and a fair regard for others' rights, if they don't stand *too* much in your own way. You can push away an obstacle, whatever it may be. You would make a good insurance solicitor or sewing-machine agent—for the company you were employed by.

You want to enjoy yourself and have others enjoy themselves, even at your expense financially, if you can afford it.

Your mind is mathematical, positive, shrewd. You are positive, courageous, not over-poetical, and apt to accept only proven facts. What you *know,* you know with all your might. You are somewhat fond of finery and show, especially if Jupiter is in Aries in your nativity. (See note No. 7 at end of readings.)

☙ ☙

March 27, 28, 29, 30, 31, April 1.

Occupations: Architect, Overseer, Building Contractor, Artist.

You have a good idea of form, outline, much executive ability, and grasp of general details, but you do not like to take short stitches. Basting is more in your line, leaving some one else to *do* the finer work. You are somewhat domestic in taste.

You are domestic, kind in your home, and patient with your own children, but not overly so with those of others. You will endure a great deal of hair-pulling at home, but very little outside. You are fond of music and poetry, but not likely to shine as artist, musician or poet. But you are a fair specimen of a good all-around individual.

You are faithful, just, intellectual, sympathetic and kind, and an originator to a considerable extent; you would make a very good and practical architect; thorough in your work. Your buildings would not tumble down, even if they lacked in the higher features of art. You have a roving disposition, and want to see *for yourself* what is going on in the world.

Special to March 30, 31, April 1.

You are a strong thinker and reasoner, somewhat opinionated, and not apt to believe everything that people tell you. You are fond of good living, rather nervous at times, and may gain the reputation—undeserved, of course—of being a crank. You have many friends. If a woman, you would make a good milliner or dressmaker, but would need some capable assistant to do the real work. Not that you are lazy—far from it—but your grasp is large, and fingers too big for fine details of production. You know when it is done, however, and still, with all your dislike for details in execution, you are not easily satisfied with your own work. You color your picture and recolor it in spots, and work over detail again and again, and sometimes have a picture unfinished for a long time, apparently unable to see excellencies that others see. There are some contradictory manifestations even in Aries, but they are apt to harmonize after a time.

☘ ☘

April 2, 3, 4, 5, 6.

Occupations: Editor, Critic, Banker, Accountant.

You have some psychic power, and are fond of the occult and mysterious. Your thinking, reasoning, imaginative faculties are marked, and you are apt to be a voracious reader. You are sympathetic and kind, a true and faithful friend, aspiring and impulsive, and possessed of a nervous organism that may cause you much suffering. You start out on an undertaking full of life and hope, but are apt to be disappointed at the outcome of it all. It is possible for you to sink down into melancholy, doubt and darkness.

You have the qualifications for an artist, but although you will be certain to familiarize yourself with the general rules of art, it does not follow that you will always be governed by them. In fact, in whatever channel of occupation your life may run, people had best let you alone, and allow you to work your own ideas out, and in your own way, if they would get the best possible fruits of your genius. You would jab the handle of your brush through the canvas if any interference became too pronounced. If you are a milliner, you would throw a bunch of flowers into the stove if your customer bothered you too much. You generally do things about right when your really artistic taste is untrammeled.

You are fond of society, if those who compose it are intelligent. But you are not fond of meaningless small talk, and you shut up as tight as an oyster if you find yourself in a circle where it is the principal thing. Your home conditions do not always suit you. While you love it, and those in it who depend on you, you need an occasional vacation.

Special to April 5, 6.

You have a caustic nature, and do not always choose your words. You will argue and fight for your rights. You have a strong conviction as to what belongs to you, and if you give up a thing it is because you choose to, not because you are forced to. You will tear the thing to bits first. If you get into a lawsuit, and are convinced that you are right, you will not give up so long as there is anything for the lawyers to fight over. It doesn't often matter who gets the spoils if your opponent doesn't. You are impulsive even to extremes, and stubborn and self-willed. You have a great confidence in your own judgment, which is not misplaced always, and are certain always that you are right—and you are not far out of the way, either, as a general thing. Your intuitions are good and the outcome of what you are engaged in is usually about right, although you are not always satisfied with the result.

You like to engage in great undertakings, but somehow the results are not big enough for your desires or expectations, although, if you are an employee, the employer is satisfied. You are artistic, quick, not a bit of a shirk, and will not have a shirk working under you if you can help it, and you generally make it too warm for such a person. You are proud and self-reliant, and keep an eye on everything. If you are in charge of a manufactory, you watch everything, from the engineer's steam gauge to a two-penny nail.

❧ ❧

April 7, 8, 9, 10, 11.

Occupations: Jurist, Head of Department, Machinist.

The brightness of this sign here seems to increase. You are always reaching out for something, not only for self but for those dear to you. If you are a business man and have a family, you want to "leave them well off." You have much mechanical ability, good intellect, strong will, stubborn determination. You want to be in the lead or nowhere. Public affairs have an interest for you, spite of tendencies and conditions that bind you firmly to home and family. You are apt to make many friends who have the confidence in your judgment that leads them to come to you for advice. If you live in a small country town, you are likely to be the mentor of the village. People listen to you and follow you with confidence in your judgment—*intuition,* if they know that there is such a thing. If a woman, you have a vein of vanity, and may be sarcastic, more so than your Aries brother. In your sewing circle meetings and neighborly gatherings you sometimes get red hot, and the parson's benediction or friendly "Good-night" does not always cool you off. You scold all the way home, and sometimes keep it up after you get home. And if some other village beauty waltzes off with your best beau, you will have your fingers in her hair before the thing settles itself.

Special to April 10, 11.

You will resort to any honest scheme to carry your point and accomplish your ends, especially if Mars is in Aries in your nativity. You can be sarcastic, critical, and overbearing, and may make enemies on account of your forcefulness. You have architectural talent; are a good financier, have much endurance, are inventive, fond of art, music and science, and if you have opportunities you will be well informed on many subjects. You may be argumentative, fond of attacking and being attacked. Your religious instincts are strong, although running in intellectual channels. You seek to prove your deductions and conceptions, which once established, you hold to firmly. You have the talents for money making, and have much cunning and shrewdness in this direction. Fiery and forceful by nature as you are, you have a vein of tenderness not always suspected. You can be a dangerous enemy, but magnanimous and kind to a conquered foe. And you stick to one who is friendly to you, through thick and thin, even if no one else has a good word for him. You are fond of fun and frolic, a capital companion for a picnic. You are always sure of a host of friends whether you are man or woman. You also have a streak of vanity in your make up, Mrs. or Miss Aries, which runs through your moral nature. *You are sure you are good.*

❧ ❧

April 12, 13, 14, 15, 16.

Occupations: Attorney, Judge, Financier, Salesman.

You are fond of society, and not averse to making a show. You are not fond of hard work, but had rather direct operations. You weigh everything before you adopt, or enter into it. You want home happy, and make great efforts towards that end.

At times you have strong leanings towards the spiritual—a desire which increases with age.

Absolute and quiet rest will become a necessity to you as age comes on. While you generate much power, and draw much to you, you are apt to expend more than you gain. You can keep this up for a time, for you start with large capital in this way, but you cannot continue it forever. And perhaps some rest along the way in earlier years, may bring a more satisfactory and enjoyable eventide. And this admonition is of value to every Aries person, of whatever degree of the sign. You have great scientific ability, are quick in thought and action, secretive, and a good planner. You stick to what you undertake. You are a great home lover, but not averse to changing your location. You are not fond of manual labor, but will load yourself to the water line with responsibility. You calculate closely, and count the cost before starting, but you are willing to carry the whole responsibility after you decide.

Special to April 15, 16.

You have some thought of spiritual things, but you will not let the flour barrel get empty while pursuing your investigations in that line. Material affairs seem to lie more within your province, and although after looking out for the Sunday dinner on Saturday night, you find a certain enjoyment in looking towards unseen and spiritual things, and perhaps go to church after reading the Sunday paper, Monday morning finds you ready for the world again.

You have deep insight into things, and are not afraid to enter into undertakings the outcome of which may appear to be dark and doubtful. You seem to be able to push things to a successful issue, and the light increases as you press on. You may, however, suffer through nervous strain. You are susceptible to the opinion of others, and love to be well thought of. Your sympathies with others' conditions may cause you trouble and unrest. You are apt to overload yourself, and blame yourself for happenings for which you are not responsible. You will not escape some sad and unpleasant experiences, but they will probably be of short duration. You like to have your good deeds known of men, and are not apt to "do your alms in secret." You enjoy good stories, and can tell them to perfection

You are apt to drive your projects through to completion,

even if the happiness of others is sacrificed. You don't mind your own disappointments, and don't see why others should be more sensitive. To you the world seems crowded at times, and if an occasional victim gets pushed under the Juggernaut of business needs, you consider it one of the inevitable conditions of civilization. But you will put your hand into your pocket to help his family, and stop long enough to say, "Poor fellow!"

❧ ❧

April 17, 18, 19, 20.

Occupations: Teacher, Designer, Musician, Dressmaker.

April 17, 18.

You have moods of happiness and unhappiness. It is not advisable to approach you with any extraneous affair when you are about your business, whether that may be of superintendent of a cotton mill, bank cashier or president, or housewife, engaged in cleaning house, or doing Saturday's cooking. Your sympathies expand and contract according to conditions. You are all well enough when people learn your peculiarities, but previous to that education, your best friend may thrust his hands into a thistle bush if he breaks in on you in an inopportune manner. You may affront him by suggesting that there is a proper place and time for everything, but he gets over his chagrin when he calls on you with his petition after supper.

You need much love, and you give much. You can stand some flattery. You can get very angry, but it causes you much unhappiness if you give way to this feeling. You have a great love for the mysterious, and a strong scientific leaning. You are insatiable in your desire for knowledge. Your psychic qualities are marked, and you also want to know what is going on in the world. You are fond of home, and affectionate and demonstrative in your affection. Your nature on the whole is a happy one, and you generally manage to get some comfort or benefit out of every experience in life. You are fond of travel, particularly on water.

You are intellectual, intuitive, psychic. You are never entirely satisfied with yourself, whatever you may attain to. There is something more you want to know, or some further explanation of the meaning of things. You are fond of music, may excel in this art, and are generally successful in your undertakings. You have a certain faculty of getting about what you want, if your want is not too extensive. You like everything nice, tidy, tasty, and, if a woman, you can work any old garment over into a new dress, with new effects, so long as there is a thread of it left, and then get a dress for the baby out of the remainder. If you are a milliner, you do not need to lay in a new stock more than once in five years. All you want is a pattern magazine and the old stock blossoms out again, and no one knows but that it is fresh from Paris, unless you tell them, which you don't often do. But you may let out the secret to a friend, for you like to be considered a genius. People sometimes wonder how you manage to get such fine clothes with your limited income.

April 19, 20.

Man or woman, your tendency is toward public rather than private life. You are somewhat easily influenced, but sometimes show much determination. Aries is the sign of the ram, and a drove of sheep is very easily driven when some old bell-wether is in the lead. But sometimes some more positive male member of the flock drops his head with a—butt, and things go his way for a time. You like praise better than blame, and are always ready to show how your way was the best, if the cart did upset while you held the thill.

Note: Before leaving the consideration of this sign there is a word of caution to be given. A characteristic of this sign is the tendency to wear out the thought power. Everything the Aries person comes in contact with must pass through the crucible of the intellect, and he is apt to fill the retort with not only too much of a thing, but too much of many things at once. Rest and repose is a necessity to nearly every human being, but the average Aries person rarely takes either until over-strained and outraged nature rebels, and then it may be too late. Watch signals before your train runs into the open draw, —it may be useless after the catastrophe.

Sign of Zodiac ♉ TAURUS

Begins April 22—Ends May 21

GEM: MOSS AGATE. COLORS: YELLOW AND RED.

April 21, 22, 23, 24.

Occupations: Physician, Nurse, Bookkeeper, Farmer, Cook.

April 21, 22.

You have a tenacious nature and make up your mind definitely and positively. You are generous, and fond of good things, which you like to share with your friends. You like to spread a good table, and call in as many as you can to sit around it. Those in whom you take an interest are peculiarly fortunate,—they will never want for anything while you have enough. You aim high, but if conditions tend downward, you can dive low. Sex impulse is strong with you, unless planetary conditions modify it, and you are likely to make an unhappy marriage, if not careful. You are fearless, busy, dominating, and apt to be argumentative. You belong to the class of people who "know it all," and are apt to make your advice to family and friends an infliction. You like fine things to wear, and if you have a surplus, you distribute it lavishly to your friends,—not enemies, and you are apt to have a plenty of the latter. Your pugnacity is large, and you are not prone to see much that is commendable in those you dislike. You can make money if you give your mind and effort to it, but make it more easily than you save. The time of need does not loom up very vividly in your mental horizon. This is apt to be true of all Taurus people.

With all your positiveness you are at times likely to be too easily led and influenced by the minds and wills of others, and if your leader's thought and aim has a downward trend, you may follow. You should act from your own higher intuitions, and lay your plans before getting out of bed in the morning, for your thoughts and actions are strangely influenced and affected by others. It is almost useless to argue with you when you are indulging in fierce discussion, but any one with strong will and determination can convince and carry you anywhere by waiting patiently and silently for your flow of language to run itself out. You are not always so positive and tenacious as you appear when you are excited. You positively believe a thing *while* you believe it, but it is not a difficult matter for you to change your opinion and persuasion. (See note No. 1 at end of readings.)

April 23, 24.

You are shrewd and decisive when you act yourself, but you are swayed by others very much, and much against your own will. If you wish to succeed, make your plans for the day before you get up in the morning, and are influenced by the minds of others, and then stick to those plans; only make them carefully and *think* them out, and do not forget that you are not the only person in the world. You are very direct in speech, and lose friends in that way. You are not over-exact in planning or laying out. You are quite fond of attentions, ease and comfort. You are sometimes daring to the verge of recklessness. Your aims are apt to be worldly, and sometimes miscarry, to your infinite chagrin.

You are apt to look under the surface of things; are passionate, stubbornly and dogmatically religious if you take a turn that way. There is no creed in the world like your own, in your estimation, but it is doubtful if you fully know everything that your creed involves. Sometimes when you do examine it thoroughly you throw it aside like a worn-out garment and adopt another, which you hold with equal tenacity. Some sort of formulation of thought seems to be a necessity to you, but by the time you get through with mundane affairs, your various religious conceptions would make an interesting crazy quilt, for they do not lack for color.

❧ ❧

April 25, 26, 27, 28, 29.

Occupations: Tailor, Upholsterer, Physician, Nurse, Warden in Hospital.

April 25, 26.

Sometimes you show a peculiar fitness for the occupation you have chosen, and then your talent shines. You get out of it all there is in it, and it also gets out of you all there is in you, and that is no small amount on either side. You believe what you do believe with all your might, and if you do find your place and stick to it, this devotion grows on you. You are not very parsimonious, or even saving, when money comes in easily, but you can preach an eloquent sermon on prudence and economy when the two sides of your wallet touch each other.

You have a strong will, and more than average intelligence, and can adapt yourself to any condition in which you find yourself, and if your labor is for those you love, you perform your duties faithfully and uncomplainingly, *while you are at them.* But you bring your business home with you and live over its annoyances there, and fume over them there. You are too politic to do it in the office. Learn to avoid doing this, and ultimately overcome your troubles quietly and alone.

April 27, 28, 29.

You sometimes make sudden and unexpected changes. You drop one employment and vault into another without any interlude, and generally succeed in the new one. You like to beautify your home, and have harmonious conditions about it, although you may not always enhance this harmony by your moods or words. For one reason and another you stick a great many pins into people.

You are a sort of puzzle in a way, in this, that no one can tell exactly how a suggestion will strike you, or a piece of work suit you. You may be easy to please, or nothing will suit you.

You are sympathetic and kind, and can show yourself capable of great self-sacrifice. You are, or can be, very secretive, reserved and quiet about your affairs. You love reading, and may be an earnest, effective talker,—always with a tinge of dogmatism. Your intuitions may amount almost to inspiration, and you are apt to have religious inclinations and denominational affiliations, which are strong and intense,—*while they last.* In some things you are apt to go to extremes. Learn to avoid extremes. You are a Taurus type. Study the entire sign through, and it will benefit you.

April 30, May 1, 2, 3, 4, 5, 6.

Occupations: Baker, Broker, Confidential Secretary, Warrior or Soldier.

April 30, May 1.

You are physically strong, or at any rate have much endurance. You love ease and comfort, and hate hard work, but you will buckle down to it as though you liked it. You are fond of music, art, and poetry, but rather in a mechanical way. You are much interested in the mysterious, but are skeptical to a great degree. You have a strong will and great tenacity. You show much calculation, and are apt to lay your plans well. You are courageous, but you know when things are going against you, and while you may utter a prayer for help, you keep on fighting, just as the Duke of Wellington, when getting the worst of the battle of Waterloo, while straining his eyes for expected reinforcements, cried out, "Night or Blucher!" but kept at the fight. And, by the way, Wellington was born on the night of April 30. You should have great powers of endurance, but you are not given to overtaxing them. Still, if the necessities of family urge you on, you will labor with all the patience of the ox, and not kick at the goad. You are to be depended on where emergency calls, and no one can fail to appreciate the friend who responds to an urgent call.

May 2, 3.

This part of Taurus gives much literary ability, and considerable originality. You are close-mouthed regarding your own affairs, and although devoted,—for a time,—to friends and acquaintances, you are apt to make the circle small and circumscribed. Under more or less provocation you can indulge in some bitterness of speech. You can stand a certain amount of flattery and consideration for your feelings, but you may not render as much as you like to receive. There is some pessimism in your nature, which, although it sees the brightness under the cloud, still is conscious of the cloud being overhead. You have the faculty of being intensely sarcastic in your arraignment of wrong actions, and evil-doers. Judiciously employed, this is a powerful battering ram for the demolition of injustice and oppression, and a weapon against evil in high places, that is irresistible. Marie Corelli, one of the world's literary geniuses, who was born May 1st, possesses this gift in a marked degree. She is poetically sarcastic in her language when depicting the hypocrisy of society, and her "Romance of Two Worlds" has induced more people to think along the pathway of higher thought or self study, than any other novel ever written.

Your undertakings are often conceived in and covered with a veil of mystery. You may perhaps have and keep your secret, but everybody knows that you have one. Unselfish in a way, your aim is generally for home and family, but you are not often absolutely satisfied with conditions. You love your home, but are not perfectly happy in it. You are apt to consider that your efforts are not appreciated, and if this feeling is indulged in, it may result in a mental fermentation that partakes of the nature of vinegar. (See note No. 2 at end of readings.)

May 4, 5, 6.

You are witty, original, willful, sympathetic and kind. Most of your unpleasant conditions are of your own generating. You keep rather close-mouthed, but go around with a certain mysterious air of knowing something that you won't tell, that is a billboard advertisement of the fact that you are up to something. Your imagination is strong, too much so sometimes. You are fond of dress, but in your own private room may not be over-precise in your exterior appearance. Few get into that sacred precinct, however. You need much affection and flattery, but don't always give much of that sort of thing, especially the latter. You are poetic, musical, in a sombre sort of way, and love harmony, but your psychic sensibilities get sometimes much mixed, and it is generally your own pudding stick that does the stirring, and as your implements seldom go out of your own hand, it is easy for every one to know who does the stirring. You don't always remember that what disturbs you may disturb others, and Taurus people often learn valuable lessons through the lex-talionis, if you know what that is.

You are idealistic, artistic, a lover of the beautiful, but you do not find it easy to get within reach of your ideals. You try to carry everything through with a rush, and fiery determination; a sort of bayonet charge, when a cotton wool club would be far better. You are always looking for interference or a fight. You don't always use good judgment, and try to bang along with a basket of eggs in much the same way as you would handle a basket of green apples, and so smash things—*your own generally*. And then you go looking for sympathy which you do not get, and which would be detrimental to your real welfare if you did get it. (See note No. 2 at end of readings.)

❧ ❧

May 7, 8, 9, 10, 11, 12, 13, 14.

Occupations: Actor, Stage Manager, Decorator, Artist.

May 7, 8, 9.

You have much persistency, stubbornness, and audacity;—are shrewd, and with an eye open to your own interests. You have spells when you are hard to please. You love sport, the theatre, social entertainments and public gatherings. You are mathematical, have good calculation, and capabilities in many directions. You take account of things before you move, but sometimes move the wrong way, which causes you much chagrin, annoyance, perhaps permanent sorrow. You are very abrupt at times, and prone to regard the sins of others as peculiarly heinous. If you have any comments to make on the actions of others, if they do not comport with your own ideas of propriety of morals, your language can be markedly acrimonious and uncharitable.

You have a good opinion of yourself,—and not absolutely unwarrantable, it may be,—for you have some fine traits, as you are perfectly aware, and you will therefore pardon this complimentary suggestion. You are rather hard to please, but you show much affection. You are pleasure-loving, fond of theatre, and games. You are capable and precise, and lay your plans with much judgment, but it grieves you when they miscarry, for it seems a reflection on your discretionary powers. You need to learn to take defeat gracefully, as though you rather enjoyed it, like the gambler who said that "next to winning the best fun is losing, and next to losing, looking on."

You have a quick eye to your own interests. You are affable, pleasant, politic, because it pays you to be so. You have fine taste, an eye for the beautiful and ornamental, and know how to decorate yourself, and others, so as to bring out the attractions and hide the defects and blemishes. Don't mistake the meaning of this suggestion,—there is nothing deceptive in combing one's hair so as to hide the bald spot, or even padding for the sake of beauty of outline. Nature does not plant rose bushes or flowers everywhere, but leaves something for art to supply, and you are a genuine artist in this direction.

May 10, 11.

You come under the most versatile division of this sign. You are a great reader, and desirous of information on all points. You have a judicial mind. Other conditions favorable, you should possess great physical vitality. You are a lover of music, poetry and art, and loving and just in your home relations. You desire beautiful and artistic surroundings. You are easy-going and fond of amusement, and very social. Still, you are subject to spells when you show great irritability, and want everybody to keep out of your way. You are likely to be bitter in your hatred, and demonstrative in your love. Your mind is lucid and clear, and your conversation agreeable and interesting, and arguments logical. You are quick in movement, not patient always with those who get in your way. You are sensitive to what is said and done, and want to know what is going on around you. You are apt to make many business changes, always looking for some betterment of condition for self and family. You are fond of travel, and have the faculty of making many friends. You have a positive nature, can adapt yourself to any condition, and stick to a purpose or principle. You are sarcastic and cute, sometimes sly in business matters. You want to know what is going on in the business and literary world. You want to know the opinions of people on various subjects, and want them to know yours. You work to make your home beautiful, and study out new methods of decoration. Man or woman, you are an ideal florist, and your garden or hothouse will show the variety and richness of form and color that charms the senses. You are on the lookout for developing, improving, mixing varieties, and always produce something beautiful and unique. But you are very irritable sometimes, and quite bitter in your dislikes. This is your worst failure. You can be very loving and kind to those of whom you are fond; enlarge your borders and take more into your love, and thus starve out hate. Look for, *and find* some good in every one. You will appreciate this suggestion later on in life, if not at present.

May 12, 13, 14.

You have the capacity of becoming a successful teacher. And

bear in mind that this whole world is a school. Your intellect is shrewd, keen, and you assimilate what you learn. It becomes a part of your thought life. Don't be too sensitive to what people say or think of you. Set your own standard and adhere to it, as you can, and let the world wag as it will. Everything may come your way in time.

You are rather given to change, always looking out to better your condition, but you don't always succeed. It does not pay to pull up every plant as soon as its shoot appears above ground, expecting to improve it by transplanting. You love travel and gain much in this way, for nothing escapes your observation, but however extensive your voyages, you should have a home port as an anchorage, to which you belong and from which you hail.

You are quiet, somewhat reserved, have good mechanical ability, see the uses of the various parts of a thing, the relation of one thing to another. You would make a success in the legal profession if you kept in one place long enough, which for your good you should learn to do, as you have ability to accomplish success and can do so by simply sticking.

☘ ☘

May 15, 16, 17, 18, 19, 20, 21.

Occupations: Broker, Politician, Farmer, Stock Raiser, Police Detective.

May 15, 16, 17.

These degrees of Taurus are apt to produce cunning, scheming, shrewd, calculating natures, that may conceal their purposes at the beginning, but are likely to let everything out before they put their intention into operation. Born under these dates, you are apt to go to extremes in order to accomplish your purpose, rather looking to your own benefit than to that of others. You are apt to take much pride in what you accomplish. Your principal aim seems to be your own benefit. Don't let this desire give the entire color and quality to your life. Some happiness is reflex,—it springs from happiness of others which we have made possible. Remember this.

You are apt to look at a thing through a long tube,—you see just what your tube allows you to,—which may be all true and good, but you cannot see the surrounding things. Throw down your tube and take an enlarged, a wider, view, with both eyes open, and you will grow and expand in every way. Throw away the tube.

You have a careful, well-balanced, discriminating mind, and much executive ability, combined with strong will. You are shrewd, inventive, cautious and of excellent judgment. People ask your advice and follow your lead. If you buy stocks in any enterprise, others do the same. If you plant a certain line of vegetables, your neighbor will likely do the same. If you have disagreeable habits, those closely associated with you are very likely to be influenced by them. You are a leader, and if you choose a particular breed of cattle, it will become the fashion. If you are a woman, you generally set the fashion for your village. You lead in social life, and, if a resident of a country village, you will be president of the sewing circle, or head deacon in the church, if your tendencies are in a religious way, and policy, if no other consideration, will help this tendency. This does not imply hypocrisy on your part, for people do not trust a hypocrite. A man may have an eye out for his own interest and be an honest adviser or competitor, a warm, helpful friend and associate. (See note No. 2 at end of readings.)

May 18, 19, 20, 21.

You are sociable and like to entertain people. Societies, social clubs, village fraternities like to meet at your home, whether you are the master or mistress of it. You like to make a good appearance, and your friends like to help you make one, especially as they get much enjoyment out of the occupation. You are the manager of the church fairs and bazaars. With the best intentions in the world, you are sometimes bitter and sour, especially if some one tries to crowd you down from the head of the class. Learn to take crowding with a smile.

You have not the forceful, determined, overcoming nature that so strongly marks the other degrees of Taurus. You are apt to be slow, hesitating by nature; but venturesome and ill-advised in business and social affairs. Still you may show much energy in the pursuit of results if planetary conditions stimulate you. You are fond of music and art. At times you are quite impractical, and may have a fiery temper, especially if Mars is in Taurus. Your outbreaks are apt to be sudden and unexpected. It is difficult to know just how you will receive a suggestion or any advice, as is true of all Taurus people. You are loyal to home and family, but may be fickle in your friendships. You are fond of children and have rather a jocose trend. You are social in your tendencies, fond of a good time and good company. You are rather quiet; slow in thought and decision, but very energetic when you overcome your inertia. You are somewhat impractical; fond of music and art; need much love; are sensitive to neglect; have a violent temper, explosive at times. You are fond of fun and joking; loving in your home; fond of children. In fact, when things move smoothly with you, you are a pleasant and desirable neighbor, associate and friend, dependable, loving and helpful.

You are somewhat fickle and go to extremes, although generally loyal to friends, especially if they are useful to you. You have somewhat of a nervous nature, take offense sometimes at slight causes, and render yourself and others uncomfortable. You are fond of sport and amusement, rather reckless in a business way and sometimes apt to shock the conventionalism of people, but not often doing much harm.

Sign of Zodiac ♊ GEMINI

Begins May 22—Ends June 22

GEM: BERYL. COLORS: LIGHT BLUE AND WHITE.

May 22, 23, 24, 25, 26, 27.

Occupations: Publisher, Author or Authoress.

May 22, 23, 24.

These dates lie under the cusp of Taurus and Gemini. You have great possibilities, and nature has lavished many gifts upon you, but you can scatter them lavishly, and waste them uselessly. You are a thinker, but often lack continuity of thought, purpose and affection. You are of those who can be helpful, busy and kind, and with equal facility be indolent, unkind, ungrateful and cruel. Cultivate the former. Poverty grinds you sadly, and unless you have enough to gratify your desires you can be dismally unhappy. Try to adapt yourself to conditions. Ever strive to reach your highest ideals. If a woman, you are apt to be nervous and hysterical unless this disposition is overcome early in life, and if a man, careless in manner, loud and eccentric in voice and behavior. You are proud; unwilling as a general thing to accept favors, or receive assistance, and yet, although galling to your pride, can accept favors. You seem to have two natures that are opposites, and unblending. The Gemini woman can set her friend and benefactor on a pedestal, and worship him as a god today, and throw him on the junk heap tomorrow. (See note No. 3 at end of readings.) You are apt to be an extremist in any direction in which your mind leads you. You are full of vivacity, and anxiety, uncertain at times which way to turn, but following in a headstrong way the impulse of the moment. Fear and doubt rule you at times, but with all this tendency you can be capable of heroic attainment and self-sacrifice, and stand boldly for the right. Which you will do depends entirely, humanly speaking, on yourself, for it is hard for any one to sway you against your own will. If you elect to cultivate gentleness and kindness, no one can excel you in this direction. On the other hand none can be more coldly or deliberately cruel. Remember this and cultivate gentleness. Set a high valuation on your own abilities, and associate with the refined and true, and make yourself worthy of their association. Marriage is a grand seminary for you if you enter into it through unselfish love and devotion. There is no such word as fail in your lexicon if you are true to your higher instincts, and master or mistress of the lower. You are magnetic, hypnotic and clairvoyant. You can be charmingly fascinating, and dearly loved by all, if you so will. You are enthusiastic in whatever direction your thought leads at the time. You love music and science, but unless you concentrate your efforts more strongly than you are likely to, you will not excel in either. You would make a good writer of light, volatile literature, and might excel in the deeper mysteries, did you not, like a cork, rise to the surface and float there. One thing, however, holds you firmly—the love of the good things of the world, and high position.

May 25, 26, 27.

At times you may be impractical, very fond of pleasure and gayety, devoted to sports and amusement. You are apt to be extreme in your likes and dislikes, and change from friend to foe very easily. It does not take much of an effort to switch you off from your track. Learn to be firm. Whether you will run on a new line for a great while is a problem. And you may get sidetracked. Look out for this and keep on the main line.

You may meet many annoying experiences through a certain carelessness as to results, and may get involved in unpleasant conditions through your conceit and self sufficiency. You are a poor subject for flattery. You can learn much by observing the faults and shortcomings of others, and considering them as your own, looking at them as reflections of what you might be yourself. Don't be too bitter in your criticism of those who exhibit undesirable traits which may be deep-rooted in your own nature. You are light-hearted, sympathetic to a degree, and need love. The surest way to win love is to be loving, for whatsoever one sows shall be the reaping. You are apt to make some strange blunders. You have some strong friends but you can make them many. Try. (See note No. 2 at end of readings.)

May 28, 29, 30, 31.

Occupations: Reporter, Critic, Reviewer.

You are generally well satisfied with yourself, not always, however, with good reason. You are somewhat conceited, and love praise and flattery. You have great regard for wealthy people, and love to mix up with "people of quality." You dress neatly, like pretty surroundings, and are fond of your family. You are volatile, have a bubbling over of good spirits that makes you a very charming person at times. You are quite fond of flattery, which like candy, is not always good for you. Still, if one would desire to lead you in the higher ways, a certain amount of praise is absolutely necessary. Too much critical nagging would turn your natural sweetness to vinegar. For this reason a Virgo monitor is ill-chosen. Gay, imaginative, dressy, social, you desire beauty in your home, but are apt to be fond of new places and scenes. You can be led by commendation, but criticism or blame seem to shatter you, that is, if you let it. Heed your promptings. Rise higher. You are rather close in money affairs, but will spend money on yourself and family lavishly at times. You love your children and kindred, but your affection does not always run in very deep channels, outside of your own family. Cultivate universal love. You can keep your own counsel, and if you suffer through your own acts, no one is apt to be the wiser for it, which is good.

You are very fond of dress, and want to dress your children well. Nothing is too good for you or them. You are domestic in your tastes, but are fond of public or society work when you can be conspicuous in it. (See notes No. 1 and No. 2. at end of readings.)

❧ ❧

June 1, 2, 3, 4, 5.

Occupations: Writer, Publisher, General Literature, Musician, Artist.

June 1, 2.

You are quiet, though venturesome, with the faculty of finding some satisfaction in any and every condition. You are musical, inventive, original, poetic, to a marked degree; faithful, hopeful, intuitive. You are independent, fond of home and family, to which you will sacrifice your convenience and comfort if necessary. You suffer much at times through disappointment. You are loving in instinct, and can adapt yourself to home circumstances. At times your anger is bitter and cruel. Your literary ability is above the average, and you are proud, circumspect and ambitious. Generally cheerful, musical, somewhat volatile, at times brilliant, you have periods of deep depression, but you do not make any exhibition of them before people, nor let the public suspect what is going on. You seem to be drawn two ways at once. Pythagoras likens the human soul to a chariot to which is harnessed one black and one white horse, and both pulling in opposite directions, one up and one down. You know what this condition means, for Gemini illustrates it more than any other sign. Don't get discouraged; it is the black horse only that needs the whip, his mate heads in the right direction. Take this as some compensation for the punching which your sign seems to be getting. (See note No. 2 at end of readings.)

June 3, 4, 5.

You are venturesome to the verge of recklessness, at times, but generally careful and cautious. You look out to keep out of compromising situations. New undertakings look bright to you, but do not always end to your satisfaction. You may become melancholy under defeat and disappointment, but that shows weakness. Some buffetings are absolutely necessary to every one, and the study is to get all the possible good out of them. The honey bee has a sting, but he makes a rare delicacy for the palate. And he does not use the sting unless his operations in that line are interfered with. Perhaps our resistance to higher leadings may account for many stings which we get.

You are a business character, and look to make your talents and accomplishments pay money. Many of your class are music teachers or popular artists. You are more loyal to your friends than some Gemini people; quiet and reserved, with a certain amount of inquisitiveness. You are apt to change your opinions in a very sudden manner, more by inner intuitive action, which may or may not be correct. Intuitions are valuable, but they want to be proved and checked, and verified by the higher law of love, and you know just what that means, Mr., or more particularly Miss or Mrs. Gemini, for your nature is not devoid of a strong affectional principle, by a long way.

You have marked literary ability, a vein of causticity that makes people want to keep out of your way sometimes. This trait is not a desirable one, especially in you, for you are in no degree fond of harsh criticism when directed towards yourself. Think this over, and remember that what you deal out to others is certain to be dealt out to you. If you cannot eradicate that trait, and it may be difficult, plow it deep under the soil of your nature, and make a fertilizer of it. It has a use, doubtless—everything has. (See note No. 2 at end of readings.)

❧ ❧

June 6, 7, 8, 9, 10.

Occupations: Clergyman, Tutor, Inventor, Musician.

June 6, 7.

You are forceful, but quiet and tardy, a somewhat profound thinker, with a love for justice, truth, harmonious conditions. Your beginnings are quiet and sedate, but your undertakings feel the influence of your force and energy before they terminate. You are lucid, intuitive, but governed in your estimate of things more by impressions than by calculating reason. You are sometimes difficult to please, and run up against obstacles that frequently shatter, or at least shake, your determination. You desire light on everything, and are pure and clean in thought and purpose, but things fall sometimes sadly short of your ideals, and when this experience comes your way you can be very miserable and wretched. You lack some of the elasticity and spring of this sign. You are a deep lover, but home conditions are not always felicitous. Your commercial undertakings are not always successful. You have strong sympathy with suffering. You can be a powerful comforter and aid to one in trouble, and in the exercise of this activity you may forget your own misery. It is worth the trial, isn't it? Perhaps in thus helping another, you dig an outlet for your troubles. You are more true and loyal to your friends than some Gemini people. Sometimes you leap before you look, especially in business enterprises. Your intuitions do not always prove a safe guide for you in this direction. You would make a good pastor, or if a woman, a valuable pastor's wife, or head of the Dorcas Society.

June 8, 9, 10.

You are positive, shrewd, just, stubborn, somewhat hard to please, and, being rather determined, are apt to run hard against other people's angularities, and then you hunt yourself. Be sure you are right, and then go ahead slowly, and don't butt your head against an obstacle that you cannot, just at that moment, remove. Sit down and wait. The right time will come for you to act.

Your desires are pure, and you have a love of justice, but you are sometimes discouraged, at your failure to accomplish your desire. Remember Joshua's siege of Jericho, and don't give up if the walls of evil and wrong do not tumble down after you have marched around them for six days. The seventh day will see them tumble. Learn to concentrate your force and energy. Learn patience.

You are a good conversationalist, and make many friends among people of prominence. Your sympathies are strong and deep, but your business talent is rather small. You are likely to pile failure upon failure if you go into business alone. Employment is nearly always best for you. You are a strong lover, not always happy, but not given to inflicting your unhappy moods on others. Possibly they may not suspect you of having them, unless they suddenly surprise you while you sit in your sackcloth and ashes. Shake these.

☙ ☙

June 11, 12, 13, 14, 15.

Occupations: Clerk, Salesman, County Attorney or Jurist.

June 11, 12, 13.

You are proud, energetic, venturesome, fearless in a measure, and ready to fight when occasion requires. You decide and act quickly and impulsively. You are conservative, not ready at all times to disturb the existing order of things. You are demonstrative, affectionate, with strong ideality. You have many friends, a sufficient number of enemies, but are not malicious nor unjust in your dislikes. You have a great regard for intellectual and scientific achievement, strong spiritual leanings, and are desirous to know and understand the hidden workings of everything. Motive in others counts more with you than act, and you are lenient in your judgment of the acts of others if you are convinced that honest intention lies beneath.

You have strong psychic power, and intuitional nature that can be highly cultivated. You are musical, poetical, and on the whole somewhat of a happy make up. You are demonstrative in your affection, sensitive, and have a marked idealistic nature. You have many good friends, some bad enemies, but not meaningly malicious, although you do sometimes let your disturbed condition have full vent, and then you may alienate a friend, or deepen the hatred of an enemy. You have your "down spells," and then you want to be left alone, except by some very close and dear friend, who gets you out of the condition.

You are wilful, determined, shrewd, penetrating, sensitive, harsh at times, but generally kind and loving, and always very sensitive. Unseen influences play strongly on you, and if you are inclined towards spiritualism you may become mediumistic. But whether you will or not, these unseen powers affect you strongly, and you have impressions and intuitions that you cannot always readily define. This is perhaps debatable ground but is apparently becoming more a matter of belief and fact, and if you have no fears to deter you, you are apt to be an investigator along these lines. The reward is great; therefore fear not. Try.

June 14, 15.

You are close in money matters, but sometimes show a marked generosity, especially towards a friend. You are given to change of residence and occupation, unless, as is apt to be the case, condition or duty hold you fixed, and if this is your condition you do not chafe much under it, for you are faithful and loyal to what you consider your duty.

You are close-mouthed regarding your affairs except with your very intimate friends. You seek advice sometimes but do not always follow it, especially if it is contrary to your own intuition, backed up by your desire. And while strongly disposed to have your own way, you will sacrifice your own desire for the sake of peace and the welfare of your family. (See note No. 1 at end of readings.)

June 16, 17, 18, 19, 20, 21, 22.

Occupations: Bookkeeper, Cashier, Accountant, Literary Editor, Confidential Clerk of more than ordinary value.

June 16, 17, 18.

You have a quiet, generally happy disposition, enjoy luxury and ease if you find them come your way, love home and kindred, have great musical taste, love poetry, but are inclined to be impractical in a business way. You look for heart sympathy, and are strongly drawn towards those who give it, but you meet many disappointments in this direction, which is good for you. You will save yourself much worriment if you can convince yourself that this is not a world of idealistic realization, nor are there many affinities found in it. You are idealistic, sensitive, conscious of struggling power within, and are subject to melancholy and sometimes doubt. You have warm and devoted friends, but they do not always find themselves able to help you out of your moods, as it is difficult for them to do so on account of your own attitude of mind when in these spells, and so you sit practically alone. Still personally, you are a valued friend, and thought more of than you suspect sometimes. Remember this and learn to appreciate your friends.

On the whole you are tolerably contented, although not by any means a stranger to reverses of some sort, which at times seem to weigh you down. Your great trouble is that you do not arise to a full knowledge of your real worth, nor understand fully how highly you are regarded by those who know you. The best thing you can do is to find out, in some way or other, that there is more true metal than alloy in your own composition, and this you have to be left to find out in your own way. Stop doubting and criticising yourself; leave that to those who don't know you. You are all right. (See note No. 4 at end of readings.)

June 19, 20, 21, 22.

With good ability in a commercial way, and more than average executive ability, you are markedly impractical. You are strongly affected by music, poetry and art. A true, sympathetic, loving companionship is a vital necessity to you, but you are not likely to find it. Even if you seem to discover it, disappointment in some form or other awaits you. Many reverses lie in your way which are apt to involve those who follow in your lead. You suffer misunderstanding and misrepresentation, and suffer patiently. You are sensitive and feel keenly any apparent neglect, although you seldom *manifest* any feeling in this respect. Sharp and cutting in speech under provocation though you may be, your friendship and loyalty is tender and deep. Although close to a certain degree in money matters, you perform quietly and secretly many acts of generosity, the knowledge of which outside of yourself and the recipient gives you much annoyance. You are artistic in tastes to a remarkable degree, and love to engage in occupations which give this instinct full play. If you do not meet with your share of sorrow and suffering, absolutely undeserved by you, you will escape the ordinary lot of those born in this degree of Gemini. Still you will have this consolation,—if you will avail yourself of it,—and do not forget that the affection and esteem with which your friends regard you cannot be measured.

You have a nature motherly, sympathetic, loving and solicitous for the welfare and happiness of others. The cares, sorrows, and misfortunes of others rest on your shoulders with undue weight. Drop them. You are scholarly, bright, thoughtful, sometimes morbidly contemplative, strongly imaginative, and of a deep religious cast of thought, although this trait will not be apt to take on a dogmatic form. Your sympathies are too broad and deep for this. You are not much given to words, but have great power of expressive language, when circumstances call it out. You enjoy wit and fun if it is chaste, clean and sensible, and can be a most entertaining companion. But in the ordinary course of events there is likely to be more shadow than sunshine in your life, and in the shadow you will seem to sit alone, largely your own fault. You have a fine taste in a mechanical way, and can originate and work out beautiful things in the way of household adornment. Cultivate this faculty.

Loving, kind, generous, imaginative, you have a vein of sarcasm that amuses your friends, for it is good-natured, witty and refined. You are apt to have deep religious convictions, but are not given to parading them. If you are an agnostic, which you may be, you are a devout one. In the working out of artistic designs for home decoration you are a marvel. Even if a man, you may be found an adept in embroidery. Your artistic taste is always coming to the surface, and your tastes are refined and lofty.

Note.—In conclusion it may be remarked that while the deeper, interior characteristics of Gemini are portrayed in this chapter with all possible accuracy, the reader may find some things not in the line of his or her observation. In explanation let it be borne in mind that there is no sign of the Zodiac more susceptible to *planetary influences,* and the apparent contradictions of the Gemini characters are largely attributable to this susceptibility. The inner and the outer are often at variance.

Sign of Zodiac ♋ CANCER

Begins June 23—Ends July 22

GEM: EMERALD. COLORS: GREEN AND RUSSET.

June 23, 24, 25, 26, 27.

Occupations: Salesman or Saleswoman in Art Emporium, Fancy China and Articles of Virtu.

June 23.

These dates are under the cusp of Gemini and Cancer, the most fickle and uncertain signs of the Zodiac, one governed by the "Volatile Mercury," and the other by the "Gentle but Changeable Moon." Stability or fixedness of purpose will be a difficulty to you of these dates. Mind I do not say an *impossibility,* for nothing is impossible. You will find obstacles to your higher development hard to remove and overcome, but this once accomplished, your victory will be the greater. You certainly are not devoid of determination or power, but your ability, disposition, perhaps, to direct and focalize this force, requires a persistent effort that may not be consonant with your nature. I mean your external nature. The fact that you are opinionated and self-willed proves the truth of this statement. Your unstableness may be a surface trait. And the charming coquettishness of your nature—my Cancer sister,—may be made of great use, for you attract and hold people, and therefore can influence them for good or evil. You are apt to be fond of display and ornament,—don't let this fondness run away with you. Those born in this sign are apt to have a time of it. So, my dear Cusp friends, the sooner you are aware of the kind of material with which you have to work, the better, so that you may get right down to business, for you are opinionated and self-willed. The only really strong point in your nature is your determination, and you should use this one strong trait to overcome these zodiacal conditions, and thereby rule your stars instead of being ruled by them, thus bringing into perfect action the hidden power within your own soul.

If a man, you are apt to sacrifice business to pleasure, and become a high liver. You are, especially, if a woman, fond of show, have a great love for display and ornament, and can go to any extreme to obtain your desires in this way. Still you are almost certain to retain the love and affection of your friends for you have a personal magnetism, at once strong and tender. If you meet with reverse some one comes to your aid, and if you are a man, it is apt to be a woman. Cultivate the true and noble, love nature, thus becoming capable of great attainment. (See note No. 1 at end of readings.)

June 24.

You are brilliant, and always appear to the best advantage. You are a good talker, great reader, but seldom go very deep into conversation. You are kindly and gentle to a marked degree and your friends find it difficult—unless the friend is a Virgo woman—to upbraid you for your conduct, even while they look with some anxiety at your peccability. You are pretty certain to have an easy swim in spite of everything, for your tender kindliness and sweetness subdues criticism on the part of your friends, and you have none for yourself. But do not forget that everything has its culmination, and if you are the parent of a child born under this cusp, watch carefully,—especially if she is a girl, for these children are often super-sensitive to the thought and influence of others, and early impressions may make permanent marks. To these natures *happy* and *congenial* marriage is a necessity.

June 25, 26.

You are kind, loving, gentle, motherly,—even if a man,—fond of home, very sensitive, and quick to take offense. You are true to those you love, intensely affectionate towards your mate, and look for the same in return. You have fine mechanical ability. You are secretive, somewhat parsimonious. fairly domineering, and like to have your own way, which,—unless you have more self-control than is usually found in this degree of Cancer,—may bring you into trouble. Acquire the faculty of being *wisely led*. The friend who may become in a way your mentor should be judiciously chosen, and you are certain to have no lack of friends. Don't give up your own conscience, but use it for testing *the advice you may receive.*

You are in search for light, and have a decided tendency

toward mysticism, which may take on a weird form. You have strong intuitive power, are passionately fond of poetry, art, music, and all elegant accomplishments. You love to teach and instruct, and are not niggardly in imparting information. Although you are shrewd and calculating in business, you do not often accumulate wealth,—if you do, some one gets it away from you. You seem to have an impractical streak, which upsets your success in unexpected ways, but if you do fall overboard you don't drown. Someone is at hand with a boat hook to pull you out.

June 27.

Your nature is motherly, domestic, soft, kind and true. But you are a dear lover of finery, jewelry and showy ornament. The Cancer woman whose tendencies are external may go to extremes to gratify her vanity. Above all things she should avoid an unhappy or uncongenial marriage. Loving and gentle in the extreme, she may be an angel to the man who can, and does, understand and appreciate her. Sensitive to unpleasant surroundings, even made ill by inharmonious spheres and environment, if she finds herself *chained* to these conditions, she must escape, or die, and she generally does the latter. And so this fact is emphasized right here, for herein lies your danger, if you are a Cancer woman put your lover's affections to the utmost test before you link your fate with his. Far better for you a solitary life, with the love of friends, than the wreck of your life by an unhappy marriage. Some women can live through this; the Cancer woman, unless phenomenally centered and poised, will find the condition almost unbearable. And don't blame *her* that she does. If you are a man, your love of finery will not be so evident. You may have poetic instincts, with rather of an agnostic, questioning, doubting quality of mind. You enjoy the company of your own thoughts, and while you are thus employed, you do not relish interruption. Your ideals are high, and you like to enjoy them, even if they have no real existence for you, except in your own imagination.

June 28, 29, 30.

Occupations: Upholsterer and Decorator in the highest planes of the Art.

June 28.

Your nature is distinctly material. If you are a father, and the mother is in any sign except Leo, the affections of your children will twine about you rather than about her. You are very fond of dress and finery, and have excellent taste in this direction. You are sympathetic, kind, and in spite of the innate changeableness of this nature, are true and loyal. You love to gain and impart information. In financial matters you are apt to be impractical. You are fond of your home, demonstrative in your love, and artistic in your home arrangements. You can twist a piece of calico into a neat and attractive ornament. Try it. Your basic nature, that colors your life, is poetry and love.

June 29.

Your sensibilities are fine and acute, and disappointment in your ideals makes you sad. You love to sit silently in the midst of an ideal world, and are happy in seclusion. At times you may exhibit a hot temper, and are secretive, somewhat covetous, and fond of appreciation and renown. You are sensitive to the conditions around you, and feel the mental and physical states of others. You are seldom troubled very deeply about things, but you are a strong lover and expect love from others. And this trait may cause you to be misunderstood, for the distinction between wild desire and real *"heart-hunger"* is not so manifest to the average mind as it might be. So don't worry yourself too deeply if you are sometimes misjudged or perhaps, impaled.

June 30.

You have much self-reliance and love to rule. Truthful and just, the spiritual nature within you is strong. You love to have the best of everything, and while you will not break your heart over the deprivation if these things are out of your reach, you will have them if you can afford the expense. You desire to be known, are fond of teaching, and are sure to be beloved by your pupils. You are loving and expect love, and you are not often disappointed. Perhaps it might not be out of place to add a word of advice to those of these two latter dates, regarding a certain sort of extravagance in idea and expenditure into which they may be tempted to enter. It may be hard for our Cancer sister to convince herself that a cheaper quality of fabric will answer her purpose just as well as the more expensive goods further up the counter. The discipline of self-control in this direction is good for her, as well as for *all of us,* in fact.

❧ ❧

July 1, 2, 3.

Occupations: Physician par excellence, but not a surgeon; Nurse, Lady's Companion.

July 1.

You are kind, loving, true, loyal, and devoted to those you love, but you have a strong will and can be domineering. You are not communicative, are independent, and can adapt yourself to any condition. Your psychic powers and intuitions are very strong and sometimes overcome you. You are a natural psychometrist. Do you know what this means? Find out, and then cultivate this faculty. You have a great love for the mysterious, and are apt to investigate deeply and fearlessly into occult matters, in which you may become an adept. At times you are quite forceful, overbearing and quarrelsome. You are fond of water travel, like to become favorably known, may be literary and are fond of the theater and drama. It is very seldom that worldly or practical things cause you much worry, although you are not absolutely careless or indifferent. It is hard for you to live a single life. Get married.

July 2.

You show much persistence and pertinacity regarding your undertakings and cannot be beaten out of your intention. But you may, by reason of the persistent interference of some busybody, who has not learned the art of minding his or her business, throw the whole thing over in disgust and never touch it again. Crablike you avoid a hole out of which you have been once routed. But you do not always show good judgment in thus being *nagged* out of a project that you cannot be *beaten* out of. It is an exhibition of weakness. When you are acting under the influence of your best judgment and intention, carry your determination through, and don't throw it up in a spirit of petulance, and don't forget you are as likely to be right as the meddler.

July 3.

You are rather silent and reticent at times, and independent. You will talk if it suits your purpose, but no one can force your speech. Your sensibilities are fine, you have a deep love for the mysterious, and can see clearly in a condition that seems darkness to many. You delve deep in search of knowledge, and spectres do not frighten you. At times you live in a world of your own, but you say little about it to others. You are fond of travel, especially by water, and have much literary talent. Possibly, if a man, you might find it well to establish more confidential relations with a select few. While the writer fully estimates the value of the "chamber within a chamber," into which but one human being may be admitted, it seems to him that one may be too much of a recluse in some matters. A man may be a part of the world, and bring light and comfort to those in need, without being swamped by it. Don't you think so, my Cancer brother?

❧ ❧

July 4, 5, 6.

Occupations: Physician (you would be eminently successful, and popular in your circle); a powerful pulpit orator.

July 4.

You are powerful in a psychic way, strongly mystic, and nothing in this or the unseen world can be hidden from you, if you determine to find it out. Investigate. "Try." You are deeply, mystically religious, and if a single man—you will be a lonely one, as *men* see. You may become a marked figure in the occult world. You can talk fluently and to the point, and your explanations are clear and lucid, but you can be reserved, and people know as much of your private affairs as you choose to let them know, and no more. You have marked self-control as a general rule. You like to be made much of, and it pleases you to have people come to you for information and advice, whether you give it to them or not, though you love to give to the deserving.

You are cautious, somewhat anxious regarding the affairs of those you are interested in, and thoughtful. You have many strange experiences in life, and sometimes a torrent of sadness sweeps over you. You make many friends, and keep most of them, and in spite of some exhibitions of your domineering traits, they never lose their deep regard for you, although they may get out of your way, temporarily or permanently. They will, however, remember that you are a sincere, earnest and helpful friend.

July 5, 6.

There are many sad experiences in your life, especially in your younger days, and you attain to whatever height you reach by toil and suffering, but the end is worth the sacrifice. You do not care for finery, but what you have in the way of ornament is sure to be of the best, and so is the texture of your clothes, although you may affect many eccentricities in dress. You are cautious, anxious, thoughtful, but the depth of your love nature only those know who come in touch with you more interiorly. *You* might gain by enlarging your borders in this direction. Come into closer touch with the great heart of humanity that is beating against your own. Never mind the little disappointments that you may experience by so doing. Don't lose faith in mankind because *men* are untrue. Remember that you and God are true.

You are sometimes taken advantage of in spite of your insight into men and methods. You are deeply wounded by the defection of a friend, especially if you have been a mentor to him, but you give no sign. You are a deep student into causes, and hidden forces, and are able to command those powers that many men fear and dread. Not many doors leading to a deep understanding of things are shut to you; none are bolted. TRY. Do you need instruction? Seek it within. All power *resides* there. You have it.

☙ ☙

July 7, 8, 9, 10, 11.

Occupations: Nurse, Teacher, Clergyman. Too honest for a lawyer.

July 7, 8.

You have a sympathetic, kindly nature, very sensitive and easily offended. You are just, regardful of the feelings and opinions of others, and generous and charitable in your judgments of others, but you are apt to get but little of this sort in return. You have some shrewdness, a love for music, are careful, and lay out your plans with admirable method, but they sometimes miscarry to your intense chagrin and disappointment. Your aims are generally high, and you have a fair measure of curiosity. Your intentions are the best in the world, but you often feel that you do not get due credit for this, and you may have periods of deep depression through the reverses that will come into every life. Do not be put down by them. You are capable of overcoming such conditions. Do it.

July 9.

Like all Cancer people you have the maternal instinct very pronounced. You are original, daring in thought, fearless in investigation. You have a legal mind, are inventive, imaginative, not easily driven. Your aims are high, and you are certain to reach them, for you have much power over yourself, and are capable of much self-sacrifice. You are not always satisfied with your surroundings, and many people with whom you come in contact disturb you. You are sometimes anxious and fearful of the outcome of your projects, but this does not often diminish the tenacity with which you pursue your ends. You are a natural reformer, and have much of the stuff of which martyrs are made. You pass through much mental suffering, quietly and uncomplainingly, very capable of aiding the world to better conditions.

July 10.

You might succeed as a lawyer, but not as a general solicitor. Your forte would be office practice, to which you would bring faithfulness, fidelity, tenacity and sound judgment. Your client could repose the most perfect confidence in your ability and integrity. But ordinary court practice would be distasteful to you. If a woman, you are imaginative, anxious, somewhat fearful, but spite of this latter trait, you may be found in the ranks of the reformers. Your sympathy is tender; you are forgiving, and if your environment is harmonious, very helpful and loving.

July 11.

You would make a good conscientious physician, gentle, sympathetic, thoughtful, but determined. Your intuitive power would be largely drawn on in your diagnosis, and you would not follow the lead of any school. You are generally "sufficient to your own need" in whatever you do, and although you listen patiently and understandingly to advice, it does not swerve you from your own settled conviction. You can indeed change your view of a thing, but this is generally by some interior light. If a woman, you are active in church or society work, and a mentor often to the young girls of your circle.

They are not afraid to come to you with their disappointments, hopes, or even mishaps, for in you they find a dependable, helpful friend.

❧ ❧

July 12, 13, 14, 15.

Occupations: Doctor, Lawyer, Clerk, Inventor, Promoter of Inventions.

July 12.

You are quiet and think deeply, as a general rule, but you have a high temper and may act under an ill-advised impulse. You have a somewhat critical nature and can be crucial and burning in your criticism. You are not given to palliating offenses against truth and right, neither on the part of others nor your own part. Your judgments are just and impartial. You have a well informed mind, are shrewd and close-mouthed. You decide questions quickly, and appear to jump at conclusions, but you don't. You accomplish much or most by dint of great effort. You love home and try to make it beautiful and harmonious. You can be relied on, and people are not slow to find it out. You are high in aim and desire, capable, and deserve all that you obtain. And "that peace that passeth understanding" leads all. Get it.

July 13.

You can be caustic in your language, when assailing wrong or injustice, but you are not apt to let go of yourself. Sometimes under strong impulse you jump at conclusions, but you quickly get back to your basis of good judgment. You have some combativeness, which you use to good purpose, and you do not prolong a fight after you have gained the object for which you fought. You do not seek any inferior position, and you are capable and deserve all you get. If a woman, you will have some pride, and a desire to have your children make a good appearance. In fact your pride principally runs in this direction. Still *you* do not want to be in the back-ground. Keep to the front.

July 14, 15.

You are domestic, loving, sympathetic. You never turn a deaf ear to any call for needed help, nor turn your back on real suffering. You may, from a conviction that some discipline is a necessity to human life, apparently stand aloof, but you are on hand when the help is really needed. You revel in the mysterious, and have psychic power that can be grandly developed.

You often labor under great mental tension, and when in this condition you retreat within yourself. You do not often cry out for help even in the midst of the battle. You seem to rest in the intuitive conviction that the needed aid will come when the time is ripe, and you have a firm trust in an unseen, but omnipresent POWER. And this trust never fails you, although you pass through some dark places. You sometimes change your occupation suddenly and completely. You are fond of travel, a keen and successful student of men and motives. You have a grand power for good, and can be very helpful to others in counsel and advice. Planetary conditions play powerfully on you, but they cannot overthrow you. "The wise man rules his stars," and the higher wisdom is within your reach, one of the great blessings to be born to man. Do not fail to develop this splendid faculty. There are ways to get into contact with those who can aid you, if necessary.

☘ ☘

July 16, 17, 18, 19.

Occupations: Physician. In this profession you would excel, and your methods be marked by originality and keen intuition. Attorney, as adviser or administrator.

July 16, 17.

The grander characteristics of Cancer are marked in your nature. You are commanding, self-willed, and capable of attaining great poise. You attract people to yourself for guidance and advice. You are argumentative, a clear and sound reasoner, generally of good disposition, but can be sarcastic and cutting. Naturally you love or hate strongly, but you do not cultivate hatred. You are apt to idealize those you love, and while, like those just previously described, you can administer castigation, you wrap something soft about the rod that you use on your friends. You have an intense desire to make people and things better, and you are of those who can, "hate the sin and love the sinner." You are fully conscious of your own innate tendencies towards human weakness, and your advice to those who seek it has a strong tinge of some personal experience. You want to do things in your own way, and if in your efforts to benefit others their own personal desires become much in evidence, you know how to stand them off and have your way, but this sort of thing brings you no particular credit. You are considered indifferent and cold, but this does not swerve you from what you consider the strict line of duty. You are appreciated by those who learn to know and understand you.

July 18, 19.

You are domestic, home-loving, a kind parent and very sensitive. You love gayety, society and dress, but you burn these desires on the altar of sacrifice if they stand in the way of your development. Your nature is happy and cheerful, but you have many anxious moments. You are apt to idealize those dear to you, but sometimes your idol gets a fall. You may have a vein of vanity and conceit that sometimes causes you anxious moments, but you will master it in time, for you do not stay down long at a time, although when you are under a cloud it is a dark one.

☘ ☘

July 20, 21, 22.

Occupations: Lawyer, Salesman, Trader.

July 20, 21.

You are quiet and secretive in manner and not always fair with yourself or others. Overcome this trait; for you are a good talker, shrewd reasoner, and apt to carry people with you while they are under your influence. And if you wish them to put implicit trust in your integrity, be fair and square, as you must know that at times you are apt to be unfair. Face about. You love dress and finery, and are bound to have them if you can without too much compromise with your conscience. You are studious, fond of books, but you do not always return those you borrow. Do it today. Still you want to be honest and true, and you make many a severe struggle with your desires, when they get too palpably selfish. *You want to be good.* You have no really downward tendencies, but circumstances sometimes are too much for you. You have the power to overcome. *Use it.* The force of desire is a potent factor in life, and your desire is for what is good and true. Labor along in the line with that desire,—*be* true as well as *desire* to be, and if your efforts towards the highest in life are as strong as your desires in that direction, the consummation is certain.

July 22.

You fit easily into almost any place. You are full of life and activity, impulsive and full of energy. Failures do not suit you, but you have them, only you do not learn everything that you might from them. You have your share of vexations, which you sometimes magnify. You have many true and loving friends, who do not think much less of you if you are sometimes fiery and combative. There is no malice nor fury in your anger, and your gentle mood returns soon. Keep cool under exciting conditions, and you will master them. *Be silent and grow strong.*

As the sun draws near to its own house,—Leo,—the more marked characteristics of the previous degrees become intensified. Purity and spirituality become stronger, if the trend of life has been directed upward, but the attraction of what lies underneath asserts itself if the current of thought and desire is downward in its flow. Secretiveness merges into trickery; love into passion; annoyances become vexations, and disappointments become calamities. But remember that with the demand of the day comes the strength from within which is equal to it, for in the arrangement and ordering of all the minutest details of human life OMNISCIENT WISDOM and OMNIPOTENT LOVE have established a perfect equilibrium,—whether we can discern it now, or find ourselves compelled to wait until the final revealment. Virgo and Libra will furnish you true friends, but your conjugal companion, if you are a woman, is best chosen from Pisces or Scorpio, if the Scorpio man has learned to overcome.

Note: In this delineation of Cancer perhaps more seriousness has been shown than in preceding signs, or than will appear in later ones. But the shadowy side of Cancer is no joke. These people pass through many deep trials in their upward course, and they are apt to conceal them and suffer alone. It is the disposition of some writers to castigate Cancer. This writer does not sympathize with this disposition. These people have their peculiarities, but they have a deep, tender, loving nature. The writer has valued friends in this sign, whose friendship has been unselfish, generous and true. And should these lines meet the eye of some of them, they will understand why his regard for people of this sign is pronounced and unshaken.

Sign of Zodiac ♌ LEO

Begins July 23—Ends August 23

GEM: RUBY. COLORS: ORANGE AND RED.

July 23, 24, 25, 26, 27, 28.

Occupations: Tailor, Decorator, Milliner, Dressmaker, Cook, Baker, Confectioner.

July 23.

These dates lie under the cusp of Cancer and Leo. And this part of Leo produces the most daring and assertive people in the world. The love of ease, so characteristic of Leo, is more or less permeated with the restless activity of Cancer. Your nature is sensational. You are always looking for some new sensation, and whether you are free and open, or secretive as a fox, depends largely on planetary influences, for Leo is a sign that is easily, and sometimes strangely, worked upon. If a man, you will demand that most absolute honesty and faithfulness from others, but it is not certain that you will give it. What you stigmatize as a crime in another is regarded as a harmless peculiarity in yourself. If you are a woman, you are apt to be more reciprocal in demand and concession.

July 24.

Man or woman, you are a splendid cook,—nearly all Leo women are fine cooks and you know how a dish will taste without tasting it during the process of compounding. You are a self-denying, loving mother, and will fight like a tigress for your children if you think they are threatened with harm, and resent any supposed slight offered them. You are intense in everything,—love or hatred,—while it lasts. Neglect or unkindness on the part of close intimates,—especially by the husband,—is apt to result in complete estrangement. You are neat and precise to a fault. Your memory is accurate and lasting. You will stick by a friend through thick and thin. You are generous in the extreme, and will deprive yourself to assist any one whose circumstances appeal to your sympathy. Spite of your intensity, and proneness to wound the feelings of your closest friends, you are a very lovable person, and dearly loved by all who know you. If a man, you are forceful, active, passionate, combative. You fight for your opinions against the whole town, and stop at nothing to accomplish your end. But you are a generous foe, and do not trample on an enemy when he is down. You have all the gustatory ability of your Leo sister.

July 25.

You are very sympathetic, kind, and loving, intensely sensitive, and fire off your temper on the slightest pretext. You are set on a hairtrigger, but your rage expends itself in one explosion, and then you are your loving self again. You have much mechanical ability in finer lines; that is, to put it plainly, you would rather experiment with the works of a fine watch than try to improve a wheelbarrow. But you can do either. You are just and generous in a certain way, but close in money affairs. If a woman, you are a neat, thorough, artistic housekeeper, and if a milliner or dressmaker, your hats or dresses are the fashion. Every woman who passes your shop stops to look in at the window, and generally this ends in their buying of you.

July 26.

You are loving, somewhat secretive, given to mysticism in thought and action, poetical and musical in a marked degree. You are somewhat impracticable, in many ways inventive, but your inventions do not decrease the cost of the thing you wish to improve, and therefore fail of general adoption. You do not know how to do anything in a cheap way, and may use expensive coach varnish on a tip cart. If a woman, you are a splendid cook, but you do not skimp on eggs, butter, or raisins. Your husband enjoys your product until the grocer's bill comes in, and then he squirms, but soon forgets his annoyance in another piece of your cake. You need to learn to save in these things,—don't be afraid of carrying your economy too far, for you won't.

July 27.

You are very excitable at times, and lose your head, and jump up and down in your rage. In your calmer moods you are a most enjoyable companion, bright, cheerful, attractive, but you have the fire in you, and when you let it out you know no difference between friend or foe. You have a grand mind. You are determined in what you undertake, and do not mind an occasional knock-down. In fact, you get up the stronger from this experience,—with less fury but more determination. Strange forces play on you and affect you mentally and physically. You are fond of travel, generally courteous to all, very affectionate to those you love, companionable, and of that type true friends enjoy mingling with.

July 28.

You are an independent thinker, impatient under opposition, a free thinker so far as your opinions are concerned, but not always so willing to grant the same freedom to others. You would rebel with all your might against any attempt to fetter your own thought, but burn the first man who openly doubted the truth of your dogma. Still there is a deep spiritual trend to your thought, and your intention is generally in the right direction. If you knock down a public idol and set your own up in place of it, you do it because you honestly think yours is better and the world needs it. And if the world disagrees with you, you are apt to get excited and make things lively. But you accomplish much good, if you are sometimes Quixotic.

❧ ❧

July 29, 30, 31. August 1, 2.

Occupations: Physician, Musician, Actor, Tragedian, Vocalist, Florist.

July 29, 30.

You are capable of attaining to anything, but you should be very careful, as you are apt to weaken your health through worry and mental excitement. You are nearly always strained up to a high nervous pitch. You are idealistic, but often find yourself sitting down amidst the ruins of your idols, and too much of this experience may cause you to lose faith in humanity and become cynical. Avoid this. Your curiosity is marked. You are fond of singing,—in fact, are often heard singing about your occupation, perhaps reciting poetry. You are buoyant and elastic in spirits, full of fun and jollity. You have strong leanings towards the occult and mysterious, but are too intense for an adept in this science.

You are passionate, but poetically and refinedly so, and anything debasing or low will quickly awaken your disgust, and turn you against the offender, no matter how dear he or she may be. You are domestic, motherly, intense in affection, with love for family, especially your children, that knows no bounds. Perhaps you may be harsh and exacting with them, but it will not answer for any one else to be so with them. You are devoted, loving, full of fun, somewhat suspicious, and have much curiosity. You are companionable, sociable, love to travel. You suffer much because you cannot find things just as you wish. You are a fighter if occasion requires.

July 30, 31.

You have great adaptability, and fit into many conditions. If you are a cook you would shine in the cuisine of a swell hotel or succeed in the kitchen of a ten-cent restaurant. Whatever you undertake, you get out all there is in it. You are fond of dress and finery, are generally happy and frolicsome, and fond of recreation. If you have not much on your mind you can lie down and bask in the sun as contentedly as a well-fed cat. When you are comfortable you are very comfortable, but you want to find dinner ready when you get through your siesta. You have no low aims,—quite the contrary,—and you like to come into prominence and notice, and are apt to succeed in this desire, for you do everything well that you set your hand to. And it is not rare to find a very strongly developed religious nature under this date, but this trait is more apt in your case to take on the emotional form. Understand that this word is not used in an offensive sense. You will be more apt to feel than think your religion. Intellectual dogmatism will not count with you,—in fact, you cannot be led by your head. Whatever becomes a conviction with you will have to appeal just to your heart. You may perhaps reason it out in your own way after that, but you do not demand intellectual confirmation like your Aries brother or sister. That you know a thing is enough,—to explain to another *how* you know it might be difficult.

August 1, 2.

You are very original, daring,—too much so sometimes, so that you invite criticism. You have a deep religious nature, but are more emotional than intellectual in this direction.

You feel rather than think. You are full of curiosity, and cannot pass a knot hole in a fence without looking through it. Not that you care very much about prying into people's business, but you want to know whether the enclosure is sown with oats or wheat, or whether there is a ball game on. Like a cat on a fence, you are desirous of knowing what is going on, without any really deep interest in it, either.

You are apt to be undecided and uncertain in your ways, expending much effort sometimes before you are quite certain just what it is that you are after. You want everything nice and tidy about the house, and are fond of changing things around. You have some business instinct, and will work hard to get money, of which you are very fond. But you do not hoard it,—you spend it freely on yourself and family. You sacrifice much to earn it, and are not afraid of working at the washtub all the morning, if necessary, for the fun of blooming out in a new dress in the afternoon. But what you get you generally earn by your own work, and you can set yourself at almost anything.

☙ ☙

August 3, 4, 5, 6, 7.

Occupations: Florist, Horticulturist, Designer, Actor, Elocutionist, Military Commander.

August 3, 4.

You have a discriminating mind, and are a keen, subtle, powerful reasoner, but more through intuition than intellect. In religious matters and tendencies a John rather than a Peter. You can be secretive, and conceal your thoughts and intention so that no words or expression of face will reveal them. When you please you can be,—to outward expression,—as impassive and immobile as a stone lion. The only way to make you show your hand is to arouse your temper and thus throw you off your guard. You can conceal the truth, if you wish, and sometimes,—when it seems to suit your purpose,—you can tell stories. In fact, in the line of thorough and persistent secretiveness, your only rival is the unregenerate Scorpio individual, and he or she can give you points and beat you at it. You are courageous to the extreme limit, but under some circumstances you *can* slink back into the jungle, baffled but not defeated. You will be heard from again later on though, for man or woman, you cannot be pushed out of the question. You are there to stick.

August 5, 6, 7.

You can be intensely worldly, but only for a time, for there is something deep down in your nature that draws you strongly upward. You have an impulsive nature, energetic up to a certain point, but you often go beyond your endurance, especially if the denial of your chief desires or needs in life has weakened your physical powers of endurance. Then shall disturbances are liable to upset you, and your really great capacity finds aggravating limits. You have high aims and aspirations, great desire to know everything especially in the realm of causation. You are strong in your condemnation of what you think is wrong, and sometimes lack charity in your judgments.

You have a strong love of justice, with marked religious inclinations. You are fond of dress and really tasteful finery, and you know how to dress yourself and your children. You can make a neat and tasty wardrobe from the contents of some people's rag-bags. And, after all, with all your neatness, cleanliness and regard for appearance, some conditions, especially continual disappointments and discouragements, may drive you to a slovenly carelessness, which is distasteful to you, but which a certain tired feeling or inertia,—the result of conditions that weigh you down,—may render permanent. You have much business ability, and your executive faculty is marked, but you are apt to break down physically. Therefore be careful. The cause of your break-down, especially if you are a woman, is the lack of that thing, so necessary to nearly every human being, but especially to the woman Leo, the love of a true and faithful mate. And a mere makeshift for this necessity will not do for the Leo woman. She gives all,—she demands all.

☘ ☘

August 8, 9, 10, 11, 12.

Occupations: Clergyman, Bookkeeper, Actor, Orator, Teacher of Languages, Librarian.

August 8, 9.

You are dominating, persistent, determined to have your own way, and not always sincere. If not a scholar, you have a forceful, deep, ingenious way of carrying conviction with you, and strongly swaying people's minds, although your influence over them may not last long after they pass out and away from the sphere of that influence. You can stand some flattery and approbation if it is genuine *and you know* that it is, but you are apt to be suspicious. You have much executive ability, and generally succeed in dominating those about you, while they are under your eye. But you sometimes meet your master. You have the faculty of looking out for yourself, and know how to get hold of the best end of the rope. People born on these dates are natural actors. If your tastes lead you to adopt the clerical profession, you will be continually acting, in and out of the pulpit, and a thorough ritualist. You will be looking for effects in everything. You wield a great influence for a time, but wear out after a while, and then people will wonder why they allowed you to lead them so. You have a vein of morose, gloomy humor, and say very amusing things, but there is a certain causticity about your wit that hurts. You are determined, and industriously work to gain your ends, but you can be intensely leisurely and inactive when there is no scheming on hand. You are fond of travel, a lover of music and art, a deep lover of family, and with a deep spirituality underneath all. You spend money freely, whether your own or that of others, and your undertakings are apt to be rather huge,—perhaps extravagant and ill-advised. But spite of all your drawbacks, and a strong Machiavelian vein in your make-up, you are a valuable and useful member of society. *Learn to be sincere, always.*

August 10, 11, 12.

You are passionate, independent, inclined to "boss," bold, courageous and always ready to fight if necessary. For you decide quickly,—sometimes without judgment,—and brook no opposition, for you have a fiery temper. But it is easy to make you see a point after the explosion is over and the fragments all swept up. You are very persevering. You would make a tasteful, finished musician, but you would want to lead the band. For you are bound to dominate, but you can be led if people do not let you know what they are driving at. You sometimes adopt another's idea, but its presentation is apt to evolve one of your own, which you may lay aside to adopt the one offered, exploiting it, however, as your own. Your reasoning powers are strong and convincing, for you believe what you are saying,—at least while you are saying it. You have strong religious leanings, but they do not always hold out. The colors will not always stand sunshine and rain. They don't always "wash." In fact they are likely to "run." You have great capabilities and often find yourself in positions of responsibility and trust, which you fill well and effectively. You have a keen sense of your own interests, and the world would sadly miss you were you not in it.

❧ ❧

August 13, 14, 15, 16, 17.

Occupations: Clergyman, Business Manager, Salesman,—of Artistic Goods,—Teacher, Nurse.

August 13, 14.

You may have a fiery temper, but it is soon over, and one whom you love can soon melt you to tenderness. You can be led, but not often driven. Have strong psychic power; develop it. Are energetic, aspiring, have no use for mediocrity, are demonstrative in affection, home-loving, social, devoted to family, are sometimes pessimistic and inclined to deep depression, which, fortunately for you, is not of long duration. Are very popular, particularly with those near you socially, who set a very high estimate on your character and ability, which you are perfectly willing that they should do. Although liable to many deep disappointments, things generally turn out fairly well for you, even if not always in the way you would prefer. You are faithful to those you love, and show them much kindness and sympathy, but have not much use for those you are indifferent about. You are fond of travel and moving about. You are not likely to stay in any place long enough to take root. You have marked psychic power, see through things readily and accurately, and can be trusted. You have good executive ability and know how to steer large interests to complete success. You may fly off into a temper easily, but are generally capable of considerable self-control. On the whole you are a very useful person in many ways. Any business enterprise of which you become the head, or controlling power, will work its way to a high and permanent place in public confidence, and stockholders will not fear their investments.

You have a nature that fits you for almost any condition, for as a general thing whatever you find to do you do with all your might. Not that you cannot indulge in repose or relaxation that may be marked by perfect abandon,—even utter tiredness,—but you generally earn the *right* to such indulgence. But you sleep like your representative—the lion—with one eye open, and if an opportunity wanders your way, while you are indulging, you are wide awake and "on to it" in an instant, and generally wake up the whole jungle, too. If you become a leader in the stock market, men don't sleep much while you are active. The small fry follow you like jackals,—and get the bones to pick. You are very loving in your home, and show it, too. If you are a mother you look out for your children, and see that they get their share of what is going. When nutting time comes, the basket you send your tribe out with is not the smallest one in the crowd. And hardly any one kicks, for if the lion's share comes your way you are not stingy. If some unfortunate youngster comes home with an empty basket, because he could not hold his own with the crowd, you fill it from your own store. And this is a marked characteristic of the Leo type. Fight as she will for the rights of her children, she will not enjoy the spoil selfishly, nor let them do it, either.

☙ ☙

August 18, 19, 20, 21, 22, 23.

Occupations: Actor, Actress, Milliner, Dressmaker, Cook, Artist, Orator or Elocutionist.

August 18, 19.

You are impulsive, brilliant, intuitive, authoritative. You have much natural intelligence that often supplies the lack of education. Generally fiery, impatient of control or dictation, you are sympathetic, loving, true. Much of reverse and disappointment lies along your path, but does not always break you down. You are extreme in almost every way. You love or hate with all your might, and if you are a housewife you push your physical strength to the limit of endurance, and sometimes beyond. You are versatile, and the ease with which you learn leads you to take hold of too many things at once. Your house does not always suit you, for nothing seems to be quite as nice, or quite as well done, as it might be. And so you are always around with broom, duster or wash pail, unless indeed you are busy with rolling pin and flour sifter. Learn to let some things go, and don't wear yourself out doing to-day what can just as well be put off until to-morrow. But you will not accept that advice. You are always afraid that your work will get ahead of you, and so you generally find yourself "cumbered with much serving." Cut it out.

August 20, 21, 22, 23.

You are impulsive, psychic, intuitive, with a thoroughly developed tendency towards rule and authority. You are reckless to a certain extent, but generally come out successful. You are willing to accept help under some circumstances, but you like to feel that it belongs to you. You give and demand love without limit. You want to do everything, and have everything done, in your own way. You are apt to defeat or defer desired results through this very trait. You are impatient of criticism,—in fact, any who essays to criticise you need be himself or herself above criticism. Any one else who assumes the role of mentor will meet the return stroke, with the certain conviction that his or her efforts have been wasted. You have much shrewdness that is not always manifested in the most desirable way. You are a great reader, decidedly scientific in tastes, and with a versatility of genius that adapts you to almost any calling. You can be anything and everything as you please. You can sink your own personality in any other one that you choose to assume for the time, and you change from one thing to another, and one condition to another, with the most perfect ease and abandon. You want everything as nice and elegant as possible, and if what you possess is a little better than another's share, it does not disturb you very much. But you are willing to share the pleasure of possession with others, and as an entertainer you are an absolute success. For you will not stay in the background, nor allow any one else to. There will be no "wall-flowers" in your social assemblies, but whatever talent there is in your company will have to come to the front and contribute to the general enjoyment.

You are quick and hasty in speech, and sometimes cruel and unjust in your judgment and criticism. You are a devoted friend and an equally bitter enemy. Possibly you may have strong religious instincts in youth, but you may outgrow them, very likely will.

Note: This sign is one of the most powerful, either for good or evil, of the entire twelve. Leo people are very apt t be misunderstood, and under some conditions terribly misrepresented. This results largely from the fact that their regeneration and growth is largely dependent on themselves and their own efforts, and the average individual does not understand this process. Most people believe little in any reformatory process that they do not have a hand in, and this sort of interference Leo will not tolerate. Leo people are not particularly amenable to outside dictation or attempted guidance, and the wise man will leave them to work out their own regeneration in their own way, which, when accomplished, renders Leo magnificently helpful.

Sign of Zodiac ♍ VIRGO

Begins August 24—Ends September 23

GEM: JASPER. COLORS: BROWN SPOTTED WITH BLUE

August 24, 25, 26, 27, 28, 29.

Occupations: Physician, Tutor, Stock Raiser, Botanist, Forester, Fruit Raiser.

August 24, 25.

These dates fall under the cusp of Leo and Virgo. You are born under conditions that make you a valuable member of society. This is the great Motherhood sign, and these first degrees unite the force and energy of Leo with the very practical nature of Virgo. You have great capacity for enjoyment of the blessings of life, and the faculty of drawing them your way. You are not so quick to take umbrage as your neighbor of Leo, and you have a better understanding of the advisability of minding your own business than the more pronounced Virgo individual. You have a desire to know everything, but that desire does not extend towards the affairs of others, and although always ready to give or offer advice, you do not often obtrude it in an inopportune moment. Your judgment in this particular is a vivid object lesson to the Virgo people born later in the sign. Whether as friend or associate, you belong to the class of helpful people whom the world sadly needs, and of which there are too few. You are a lover of nature,—in its animate forms especially,—and love to be out of doors. You are a tireless worker, deep thinker, and logical in your judgments and opinions.

August 26, 27.

You have a great deal of literary ability, command of language, are never at loss for words, somewhat loquacious, but there is always good sense and meaning to what you say. You are not given to uttering platitudes. Voluble you may be, but never insipid. You are conscientious—very. You have conscience enough for your own use, and some to spare, of which others often get the benefit. Sometimes you are easily irritated, set in opinion, domineering, blunt, but with always a kindly vein throughout. Somehow people make a confidant of you, but you don't always keep their secrets. You find them useful as illustrations, and sometimes the name slips out. You are intuitive, psychic, far-seeing, musical, generally well informed. You are a great reader, and go through a book, getting the pith of its contents while some people are reading the title-page and preface. This is a gift of most Virgo people, who make the best proofreaders, and reviewers of manuscript in the world. No error in grammar or expression is apt to escape you. But as a book *reviewer* you are apt to be too caustic. You are generally successful in business, although you seldom conduct it on a large scale without some law-suits. You are fond of the mysterious and occult, and may be a valuable pioneer in this way. It is not a simple matter to humbug you, and in your investigations fraudulent and designing mediums and pretended seers are apt to run to cover to get out of your way, for you are sure to see through and expose them.

August 28, 29.

You love music, art, poetry. You are a fine judge of painting,—generally commending fine work, but mercilessly scoring daubs. And in fact, everything in painting, literature or music comes under the realm of art with you, and you have little patience with mediocrity, and none whatever with meretriciousness. You are fond of the good things of life, and desire a full measure of comfort,—and provender. You want the best of everything in the way of material things, and will not buy a shin-bone when you can get a sirloin, nor wear homespun when you can afford silk, nor ride in the "Jim Crow" car when you can procure a seat in the parlor car. Not that you are extravagant by any means. If your circumstances hold you down to a rigid economy, you can adapt yourself to them, and still be cheerful, contented, and helpful—you are always that. But still you don't often deprive yourself of the luxuries of life from choice, nor hold your nose to the grindstone because you like the sensation. And when you do have a plenty, you share it, and often divide even your crust. You are a very desirable person on the whole.

August 30, 31, September 1, 2.

Occupations: Journalist, Proofreader, Musician, Literary Critic.

August 30, 31.

You are neat in personal appearance, fond of music, fine arts and the sciences,—of a discriminative mind, and generally quick in decision, act and word. You have a quick, but not malicious or vengeful temper. You are somewhat speculative. Possibly you are proud, very fond of home, a good neighbor, philanthropic and just. You are drawn quite strongly towards the mysterious, are a good and sensible talker, one generally loving and affectionate, especially toward your parents. You often evince a great deal of patient, unselfish generosity. Nothing is too good for your own family. You are demonstrative in affection, love your home and family, but are sometimes annoyed when they show a disposition to get in your way. You are mechanical, and inventive in a way, although more fond of copying the ideas of others than originating them yourself. You are an investigator, a rapid reader, with a faculty of getting at the pith of a book without reading it all. You are quite positive, not looking for trouble, but if forced into a fight are in it to stay.

September 1, 2.

You are very original in speech, and action, have a well-balanced mind,—with ebullitions of oddity at times,—are very domestic, motherly, and strongly attached to home and family, but this does not keep you at home if there is anything outside to investigate. You are accurate, faithful, thorough in all you do, but do not always appreciate the value of time. Sometimes you take up more than your hands can hold, and you waste time alternately dropping the surplus and trying to pick it up again. Generally,—but not always,—you are reliable, but your peccadillos in this line are always so outrageously good-natured that people laugh before they finish scolding you. But when you finish a job it is well done, and for this reason people wait for you with more or less patience. In fact, your over-flowing good-nature saves you many a well-deserved castigation, or shortens its administration. People like you, and well they may, for you are frank, and honest, and generous, and truthful,—or mean to be. You might be a successful public man—in country districts,—a village politician or official, but you are too honest and open for *city* purposes, as you are apt to blurt out your opinions and thus upset the cauldron in which the broth of more tricky politicians is cooking, when they want to see you out of the way at once.

☙ ☙

September 3, 4, 5, 6, 7.

Occupations: Builder, Machinist, Shipwright, Engineer, Watch and Clock Maker, a Skillful Artisan.

September 3, 4.

You are accurate in design and detail, know what you want to do, and go about it without much fuss. You want to know the why and wherefore, and having a knowledge of the laws of causation, you make them a part of your calculations and work. You are a true, reliable friend, and equally reliable enemy. If you have, or *think* you have, any just cause against another, it does not take him long to find it out, although your acts and language will be open and frank. You are generally contented with your lot and are not given to knocking your head against impossibilities. You can change home and business without much effort, and fall readily into new routine. What you do, you take a pride in doing well. You are faithful to your employer, and have an eye to his interests as well as to your own. You are sometimes apt to take a distorted view of things, and perhaps individuals, and criticise their motives in a blind, uncharitable way.

September 5.

Your psychic powers can be grandly developed. Remember, and develop this great gift. Your disposition is sometimes a strange mixture of sadness and brightness. You are apt to change your opinions,—particularly your religious conceptions, —to and fro, always with a basis of deep conviction, however. You are not vacillating, for surface reasoning does not count much with you. The deeper undercurrents of thought are what move you,—sometimes in opposite directions,—currents that the ordinary observer knows nothing of. But turn and beat and tack as you will, your compass always points one way, and you never throw your chart overboard. Don't let this fact disturb you, friend Virgo, for every turn brings a revelation.

Keep your eye on the star, your hand on the helm, and trust GOD and your own soul. You will come out all right.

❧ ❧

September 6, 7.—Characters with Agricultural Tastes.

You are positive, firm, determined, and your own way generally seems best,—to you. Your definitions suit your purpose, however they may strike others. You are rather conservative, —a stickler for old forms and customs. If you live back in the country you hate railways and modern means of travel. The old days of the stage-coach and turnpike were the best days, and the times when you were young were far better than the present age of hurry and drive. You may be right in a great degree, but your acquaintances will be likely to write you down an "old fogy." Doubtless you will make some enemies, for you hold your opinions tenaciously, and in town meeting you air them. You cannot see why the district schoolmaster should not work for a dollar a day,—as your farm hand does,—and six hours a day seems like a swindle of the township. And you mow your field with a scythe, rather than lazily ride on a mowing machine, even if your method finally doubles you up with "rheumatiz." But you are not being ridiculed. There are some men who are never created to move, and the screws that hold the works of your reliable old "bull's-eye watch" fast in its heavy silver case are as necessary as the spokes of its oscillating balance wheel. The world needs you, and will for a long time to come. But you may depend on one thing,—and that is,—your acquaintances seldom or never impugn your honesty or integrity. There is a large vein of inflexible justice in your spiritual make-up, and people have confidence in your judgment in many things. They might not come to you to learn how to increase the speed of an automobile, or for suggestions regarding the improvement of a modern reaping machine, but they come to you to settle their disputes as to a boundary line, or justice of a disputed claim, and abide by your decision.

September 8, 9, 10, 11, 12, 13.

Occupations: Jurist, or Any Occupation Requiring Discrimination, Research and Brains.

September 8, 9, 10.

You have great executive ability, and a keen, penetrating mind. You are intuitive and remarkably psychic. You are always in search of knowledge and information. In fact, very little happens around you, or in the affairs of your friends, that does not reach your notice. You are very thoughtful of family and friends, deeply interested in their welfare, and are apt to load yourself with their responsibilities, and herein lies a fruitful source of vexation for you. You are not always opportune with your advice, and with the best intentions in the world you are likely to become annoying to your friends, for it is difficult for you to see any one in whom you are interested make any move without obtruding your advice or suggestion, and a certain melancholy condition that may result from disappointments of your own, makes your advice sometimes pessimistic and disagreeable. Still, in this matter you are apt to be determined and obstinate, and, if not very careful, finally defeat the laudable object you had in view. This is apt to be one of the most unpleasant traits in the middle and latter Virgo make-up,—those born at the middle and end of the sign. If you wish to retain your influence and hold, or help to hold your friend up to what is unquestionably a high ideal of manhood or womanhood, learn to withhold your spoken advice, and try quiet mental suggestion. Remember the words of Whittier, "Into each life some drops of rain *must* fall," and if your friend seems to you to be making a mistake, don't forget that undue pressure of advice, especially if it becomes meddlesome, will result in more harm than good. It seems to be a law of Divine permission,—if not of Divine Providence,—that human nature must be purified by conflict with what we,—perhaps blindly,—consider evil. It is well for you to remember that after all ALMIGHTY WISDOM and LOVE is working out the problem of human destiny, and that the tragedy of Uzzah and the Ark is being daily enacted. "There is a time to keep silence and a time to speak." To you, my critical, but honest, Virgo friend, let me say, that, whether or not you accept the faith in the workings of an OVERRULING PROVIDENCE, you will eventually come to the conclusion that when advice or interference becomes distasteful and annoying it is worse than useless, and had better be withheld. I emphasize this fact here, for the reason that Virgo is very apt to overdo in this direction. No one can question your good intentions, and if you can patiently and *silently* wait for the consummation, the object of your deep solicitude will see, acknowledge, and profit by your advice and counsel. But when you crowd him or her to the limit of endurance, your use as a mentor is at an end. And this is a fact that Virgo *mothers* will do well to remember. These remarks apply to the most of Virgo people, but are not intended harshly. You may think that Virgo gets "soaked." That is all right. It is most valuable soil and worth the highest cultivation,—and irrigation. Take it in.

September 11, 12, 13.

You have a splendid mind, and abilities of the highest quality. As a judge your opinions and decisions would form precedents. You would decide honestly, firmly, clearly, and if on the bench of an inferior court, your rulings would not often be reversed, even were exceptions often taken to them. But men of your type are not often found below the supreme bench in communities where judges are appointed for their reliability and sterling qualities rather than through political influence, or flashy brilliancy at the bar. Still your defeats are many. You are very affectionate, loving at home, but you have spells when you are hard to get along with, and sometimes exhibit a violence of temper that neither you nor others can understand, and generally over some slight affair. If a child, you sometimes want to cry over something, you don't know what, and are shy and retiring, very fearful, but get over these traits somewhat later in life. If a mother, your whole solicitude is for your children. You are apt to be physically strong, and most of your ailments are imaginary. If you are really indisposed, you are apt to ransack the medicine chest and begin to swallow drugs, the most senseless proceeding for Virgo, for there are few disorders that you may have that will not yield to a period of rest, and a bowl of "herb tea." Add this fact to your already extensive fund of valuable knowledge, and the next time you are "sick" cure yourself as the cat does,—with catnip. Don't forget.

September 14, 15, 16, 17.

Occupations: Lawyer, Journalist, Author, Inventor, Linguist, Merchant.

You are trustworthy, capable, reliable. Large interests can be entrusted to your care in absolute safety and security. You have elegant tastes in everything relating to art, music, ornament. You have no love for the meretricious, nor are you favorably affected by "rag-time" compositions. The higher musical composers, Beethoven, Chopin, Haydn, and the like, are your gods, and in art, Rubens, Michael Angelo, reveal to your mind much that escapes the notice of the crowd. And in these matters you will be severely critical. With all your passion for giving advice, you are averse to accepting it from others. Your way of looking at things, your standpoint, is, in your estimation, far beyond that of any other human being, but while there may be a measure of truth in your assumption, you can, and often do, make it distasteful and wearisome by trying to convince others to see it as you do. You are economical, prudent, fond of money, but just. You want what belongs to you by right, but nothing more.

You are witty, fond of fun, mildly religious, perhaps more to please mother than anything, somewhat original, fond of active sports, and generally satisfied and contented,—with yourself.

You are loving, demonstrative, very fond of home,—especially if conditions there satisfy you. You don't stay out late at night. You have fine mercantile talent and good business judgment. You are reserved, hard to get at, and if a merchant, your counting room is fenced about with red tape. You may be found in the front rank of reform movements, and if a woman, will likely be found in the president's chair at the monthly meeting of the Maternal Club, into the deliberations of which you would be apt to bring valuable suggestion and advice, the result of your own experience,—for you are, in many ways, a model mother.

September 18, 19, 20, 21, 22, 23.

Occupations: Bookkeeper, Accountant, Cashier, Salesman.

September 18, 19.

You are truthful, conscientious, pure in nature, somewhat prudish, musical, fond of poetry, studious, mathematical, somewhat doubtful of your ability,—a trait which sometimes stands in your way. You have an intensity of nature that may mislead you, and cause you some suffering. You have a caustic tongue, with a disposition to use it at times, and you sometimes feel that you are not reckoned at your full valuation, but it does not better matters to keep people too much in mind of it. After an outbreak of temper you can relapse into a moody, disagreeable silence, almost as irritating as your wordy tirade. Fortunately it is not of long duration, but it is unpleasant while it lasts. Much of your discomfort results from your meddling in the affairs of your family and friends, and your inability to comprehend their feelings until an explosion ensues. Still, you have immense power for good. The well centered Virgo nature, when its real kindliness rules, is lovable, true, noble, helpful. Such a one,—especially a woman,—is sure to inspire affection and win confidence. You love to read, but if you are a woman of family you will sacrifice this desire for the good of family and home. There are not many loose ends about things in your house. You are precise, tidy, careful, economical, but not parsimonious. You are apt to be a model wife and mother. You are artistic in taste, but not showy, and you take good care of your things. You are apt to hoard old stuff against the time when you need it, which often never comes, and then, after a thorough overhauling, the rag-man gets it.

September 20, 21.

You are literary, original, a good scholar, quiet at times, affectionate, desirous of love, fond of finery, although you will not sell your soul for it. You love money, but are just in your dealings. You are cautious, conservative, somewhat conventional, look above rather than below your station in life for companions and associates, and generally find them. You are touchy at times, but not offensively so, and easily placated if you take offense. You like to be noticed, and are social, rather interesting in a mild, unobtrusive way, somewhat inquisitive and quite caustic in language when "real mad." But you are a general favorite and people like you. You like to go out calling when the mood is on you, but the place that satisfies you most is home.

September 22, 23.

It is a strange fact that these cusp people are strongly drawn towards those of a positive, determined nature, and equally strange that the powerful nature is for a time fascinated with the weaker one. But the fascination does not last always, and when the spell is over, the weaker one quietly and patiently sits down under the condition, and makes the best of it, while the stronger one frets and fumes and chafes.

Still there is some reason for this antagonism, for you have considerable of the Virgo meddlesomeness, and tendency to force advice on others. Every step any one contemplates taking appears to give you cause for fear. You look for some calamity or loss to ensue. And if this desire to advise or restrain brings the full measure of impatient reaction on your head fifty times in a day, you will make the same attempt for the fifty-first time, with the same pertinacity. New projects suggest themselves to you and you express your determination to carry them through, but sometimes you don't do it. Unlike Virgo people in general, while you are fond of offering suggestions, you are at the same time pertinaciously desirous of receiving them. You persist in your efforts to obtain advice, but often without success. Learn to do more of your own thinking, and allow others to do their own planning and accomplishing, and you will sail through life on a summer sea, for your nature is most lovable, and you attract the best sympathy and love of all. And by all means throw off the domination of fear, learn to be silent and grow strong. You have a certain sweetness and—well, *piquancy,* that makes you intensely fascinating, especially if you are a young girl. People, especially men, think you are perfectly charming, and you are. Whether or not this fascination is lasting, depends on circumstances. You have an innocent ease of manner that wins people to you. You never lack for lovers or admirers, but they are often like the bee among the flowers. They don't stay, but they return frequently. But your friends, especially among your own sex, always have a really tender, loving regard for you. They seldom or never lose it. You like to make a good appearance, and have considerable harmless and interesting pride, particularly if, as is often the case, you are good-looking. But you have one marked characteristic, and that is indecision, which sometimes takes the form of abject fear. You cannot make up your mind in regard to thought or act, without having some one to help you. If one of your family has a positive, domineering nature, you will be a mild reflex of that person. If the mother is a Scorpio woman, you will reflect her moods of jealousy, rage, nagging, and other disagreeable traits of that nature, as the surface of a quiet lake reflects the clouds that float over the sky, although not one of those characteristics belongs to you. The danger is that your nature is so plastic that these traits may be indelibly stamped on your character. You are faithful to duty in whatever line your lot may run. If you are unhappily or ill mated, no one will ever know it from *you.*

Sign of Zodiac ♎ LIBRA

Begins September 24—Ends October 23

GEM: DIAMOND. COLORS: WHITE AND YELLOW.

September 24, 25, 26, 27, 28.

Occupations: Bookkeeper, Accountant, Salesman.

September 24, 25.

These dates lie under the cusp of Virgo and Libra. You have fine intuitions and your psychic power is marked. You have strong and vivid impressions, but you are often fearful and hesitating. You hold back through some undefined dread of you know not what, and want advice at every step, and seek for it, but still argue every inch of the ground. You want to do just the right thing, but then everything seems so awfully uncertain. You have strong religious inclinations, much natural ability, and a good business head,—but you hesitate to trust either. And whatever you do, you often wish you had done the other. Sometimes you get excited and then lose your head. If you are crossing a street and a runaway team is coming your way, you give a hasty glance in every direction, let out a scream, and then run the wrong way. You want a level-headed and patient friend with you when you go shopping, to help you make up your mind. You, my dear lady; the men have more faith in themselves, although this delineation fits them. But there is something nice and interesting about you both.

September 26, 27, 28.

You are exact, determined, with some considerable force of character. You are honest and true, but can be stubborn and sometimes fault-finding. If any one does an errand for you, you are not always satisfied with what your messenger brings back. It is not just the quality of goods you desired. The thread does not quite match the color of the fabric you want to sew with it, but if you take the purchase back, you are likely to bring back the same parcel. You are very loving and show it unmistakably to those dear to you. But if you don't get a full measure of the same in return, you mope, but you don't often sulk. The desired caress sets you all right again,—until the next time. You live in the midst of calamities,—at least they appear so to you. The world seems cold to you sometimes,—it *is,*—in high latitudes. But it is warm somewhere. Learn to take things as they come and you will have a better time. And above all don't get excited,—it isn't good for you. *Sit down by the stove and cool off.* Don't worry about what you can't help, meet the inevitable with a smile. This advice is worth the price of this book if you will only take it.

You have some charming characteristics, and are musical, artistic, refined. You are highly psychic, intuitional, and love to skirt around on the borders of the mysterious. You are fond of the theatre, but don't adore tragedy. You take great pride in home and family, and like to have everything nice and trim. Your children are a little ahead of the general run, and the baby is "too cute for anything." You have many friends, are a good talker and not given to complaining. You are always ready to accommodate, and do many kind acts. In fact, you are a pleasant sort of person to have around. It may take you some time to do an errand, for if people are sitting on their piazzas or door-steps they like to have you stop and chat, and you like to have them feel that way, and you like to do it, and—well, *"you'll do,"* for you know just how to do it.

❧ ❧

September 29, 30, October 1, 2.

Occupations: Teacher, Bookkeeper, Salesman, Musician, Theatrical and Book Critic, Watchmaker and Jeweler, Engraver.

September 29, 30.

This sign now seems to change. The beam of the balance goes the other way. You are bold, determined and fearless. Obstacles go down before you like a log hut in the path of a tornado. But you are apt to wear or burn out your physical life with your intensity. You balk sometimes, but not through fear, or any doubt of your own abilities. That is not one of your prominent traits. You consider yourself equal to anything and go ahead with all the power on, until you meet with some physical breakdown. Even then you are not vanquished. You have much family pride. There are no people like your own brothers and sisters. You love home, but you will go a long ways from it in pursuit of knowledge. You worship father and mother, especially if you have a mutual desire for occult science and development. You are fond of gayety and pleasure, and with all your intuitional psychic power, you are very materialistic. You are foe to pretense and humbug, and a merciless iconoclast if you find out that your neighbor's idols, or even your own, are shams. Specious argument has no power with you, and any idea or theory that is not based on solid fact has little chance for acceptance with you.

October 1, 2.

You are sensitive, strongly intuitive, affectionate, demonstrative, and your home is your kingdom, and Baby rules in it, unless your mother lives with you, and then they occupy the same throne together, but rule as one. This is perhaps more marked with the woman than the man, but is true of either. If *he* drives out in the afternoon, Mother and Baby occupy the back seat, wife on front *with him,* of course. If *she* goes out shopping, Mother goes with her, and they stop in the cafe and have one plate of ice-cream with two spoons,—not indeed from motives of economy, but because they like to eat from the same dish. If two plates are served, the spoons go into each dish alternately. If the three of you go to the theatre, there is only one opera glass, and when it is out, if you cannot sit together on one seat in the street car, you wait for the next one. You are sincerely religious,—even if you don't believe all the parson says, and your disposition is generally happy, often sunny. You like sports and games, and are a patron of the ball ground. Your aim is to love, to be loved, and to be happy, but you have some trying experiences. Sickness or bereavement brings a heavy cloud over the home. You are a skilled artisan, at the head of your profession, and as a business man, shrewd and smart, but honest and reliable. There are no inferior goods in your shop.

October 3, 4, 5, 6, 7.

Occupations: Confidential Clerk, Private Secretary, Tutor, Lawyer, Jurist; perhaps Musician.

October 3, 4.

You are just, honest, shrewd, able. Reticent, thoughtful and somewhat proud, the secrets and interests of others are safe in your keeping. The master can take a nap after dinner and trust you to keep awake. You are a good talker—when you choose to talk—and you know what you are talking about. You see through everything that comes your way, but don't always let people know that you do. You are tenacious, like to advise, and sometimes dictate, and as people have confidence in your judgment and general reliability, they are willing that you should. You are just and fair in your dealings and are willing to pay all you owe, and want all you earn. You are conscientious, true, careful in money matters, a good trader, successful in your undertakings, if you do not destroy your physical system by some nervous breakdown. You have spells of melancholy, generally resulting from your physical inability to keep up under the mental drive. You are methodical, with the faculty of making your abilities *pay*. You are energetic in your demands, which are nearly always founded on justice and right. Anything like injustice wakens your resentment and indignation.

October 5, 6, 7.

You have a high order of mechanical ability, and if you are a journeyman carpenter, the finer work of finishing falls to you. You are exact and precise to every line, and can work out any detail of artistic design. You take pride in your work, and do not need that any should tell you that you are a master of your trade. If a stone-worker, your scaffolding is on the front of the building, and if any one wants to find you he does not look for you in the cellar. Your fund of general information is large, and not limited to the matters of your trade or occupation. You are no dollar-a-day man. If you are a woman, you don't go out washing by the day for a living. You will be found in the best establishment in the city, and very likely in charge of the most artistic department. But you are apt to break down through your close attention to business. Take more rest and quiet recreation. Learn to "loaf," and invite your soul to join you. You will not overdo it. And when you go home at night leave the shop behind and relax and rest. You will not cheat any one.

❧ ❧

October 8, 9, 10, 11, 12.

Occupations: Musician, Artist, Teacher, Lawyer.

October 8, 9.

Your intuitional and psychic powers are marked. You can live in a world of ideality, and are very loving and true. No one need doubt your genuineness. You wear no mask, but show yourself as you are. People learn to place implicit confidence in your judgment and rectitude. Positive and combative as you are, you attract the same sort of people, and you have many warm friends among Scorpio people. You have much originality, and know how to keep your own counsel. You never give any reason for what you think or do. It is sufficient for you that you have a reason, but that is your own affair. If you are a teacher, you are thorough, painstaking, with the faculty of making your pupils see the point you are driving at. If a bookkeeper, nothing escapes your notice, and any crookedness in accounts that you are called upon to examine, must be very deeply hidden to escape your scrutiny. You are opinionated, but you have very good reason to be so. Your own deductions are amply sufficient for you, and you do not often need advice, although you are ready to listen to it. But it must be sound and unimpeachable, or your intellectual penetration sees through it, and the would-be adviser may be compelled to accept *your* view of the matter.

October 10, 11, 12.

Your nature is marked by intuition, conservatism, with strong psychic traits, and some reserve. You have not many intimates, but those whom you do admit to your friendship, you take very close. You are rather opinionated, but your opinions are well worked out. You do not care to remain in the background. You know your ability, and are determined that others shall recognize it. You are thorough in everything, true and loyal to your friends and conscientious in all your dealings. What you do, you do in your own way, and according to your methods. You can give a reason for what you believe,—in fact nothing finds a place in your belief without a reason, and if you choose to give it,—which you don't always do, and never, under compulsion,—your definition of your position is lucid and clear. Your nature is a harmonious, well balanced one, and your plans well laid out, and carefully considered, but they are not always successful. You start many plans, and work them up to a complete end, almost, and then some one comes in and robs you of all the credit, to say nothing of the glory. This hurts you, and sometimes almost disheartens you. You love deeply, are fond of refined and good society, like to dress well, and are a dear lover of nature, especially in her solitary aspects. This is your salvation, for when you are at work you burn the candle at both ends. You do not care for grandeur in your home, but you like what you have to be of the best, and you can be a refined and tasteful Bohemian.

❧ ❧

October 13, 14, 15, 16, 17.

Occupations: Poet, Musician, Scientist, Teacher, Author, Dramatist, Preacher, Merchant.

October 13, 14.

An apt pupil. You have mechanical talents, are somewhat inventive, but in such things you are more apt to be given to amplifying and improving the inventions of others than originating. You see the weak points, the imperfections, the limitations of what others construct, and find a ready method of removing imperfections, and completing what others have left unfinished. You are a natural adjuster of incomplete or imperfect work, and never at a loss to supply just what is needed to make up a deficiency.

You are a strong lover, and you need love. You cannot go through life alone. In religious matters you are apt to be agnostic, with a tendency towards the materialistic. You accept proven fact, but are quick to see any flimsiness in basic foundation. Sometimes you show much excitability, and in this condition you may make mistakes in judgment. You want to have your own way, and generally succeed in having it. People yield to you, through confidence in your integrity and judgment, and well they may.

October 15, 16, 17.

You have great psychic power, fine intuition, strong spiritual leadings, that draw you powerfully towards the occult and mysterious. At times they are very strong. Yet you are not superstitious nor over-credulous. On the contrary, you have a materialistic vein that makes you almost agnostic. You demand a strong reason before you are convinced. But down deep in your nature is something—you hardly know what—that draws you firmly and irresistibly towards the unseen. And if there is one you love in the world beyond, this power within sometimes almost forces the gates ajar. But you are not a weak sentimentalist. You have splendid business ability, and commercial tendencies. Your strong characteristic is conscientious loyalty to duty. Excitable at times, you are generally cool and collected, and you push forward regardless of obstacles, which sometimes fall back on you. The devoted love you feel and exhibit towards those dear to you, is returned in full measure. You have a pure and high ideal of home life, and are a perfect housekeeper. Free and generous if you have the means, you allow no leaks. Money put into your hands to run the house with, will illustrate its full purchasing power, and your husband may be sure that you will not run him in debt. You are neat and tidy and want no slovens about you. The children may play in the dirt out of doors, but wash themselves when they come in, and remember the door mat.

But you have many sad disappointments which you bravely encounter, and up to the utmost limit you struggle and work against adverse fate. But continued failures and disappointments may finally break you down physically, and sometimes if long continued, bring your life to a close. The soul burns out the body, but you die in harness. When these conditions come on, you need to drop everything, and go out and live in touch with nature. Flowers, trees and running brooks are your best companions, and freedom from the conventionalisms and demands of social life may restore you to health and comparative vigor. But you are "one whom the soul consumes," and when half recuperated you are almost sure to come back to your burdens, and make a final break down, and then the end comes, and a brilliant, valued life goes out. Take the warning in season and heed it, and spare your family and friends a sad and untimely bereavement.

October 18, 19, 20, 21, 22, 23.

Occupations: Preacher, Scientist, Chemist, Superintendent.

October 18, 19.

Your nature is marked by close economy, fixedness of opinion and purpose that borders on obstinacy, with determination to have your own way, which you sometimes attain through a shrewd cunning. Your arguments are always convincing, at least on the surface, and you never lack for a plausible excuse when you make a mistake in judgment. You can always show the best of reasons why your plans were not successful. You have the ability to suffer in silence, and although your immediate friends may know that some heavy trouble presses upon you, they do not easily learn what it is, at least from you. You are ambitious, desirous of place and power,—a desire arising largely from your interior conviction that you are capable of filling the place. You love your home, and want it beautiful, but your own particular corner you want to yourself. You love your own family above everything, although your sympathy often demands extended limits. You are impatient with attempted dictation, and combat opposition or interference in your work.

October 20, 21.

You feel a responsibility that you do not care to divide, and if you succeed or fail in your undertakings, you want to do it all yourself. You know how to direct others, and make them understand your wishes and desires, and you will not quietly endure any attempt on their part to do things their way, if that way conflicts with your own. Perfectly willing to take all the chances yourself, and assume all liability if things are done as you direct, you have no fault to find with any failure on the part of your agent if your directions are strictly adhered to. But woe to the unlucky wight who essays to use his own judgment and then makes a mess of your business. You will have no further use for him. This trait saves you much trouble, for you generally lay your plans with great care, and uninterfered with they work out successfully. When you meet with defeat you are apt to become sour for a time, and while this fit is on, you are not a pleasant companion. However, everything comes out right in the end with you. You are somewhat materialistic in your mode of thought and can make a pretty thorough sceptic or doubter. What you believe must rest on proof,—and you like to prove things for yourself.

October 22, 23.

You are thoughtful, excitable, nervous, and liable to go to extremes, but you have more power of endurance than most Libra people. You do not break down so soon, nor is your giving out so gradual and intermittent. Your finish is apt to be more explosive, and then your first necessity is to pick up the pieces—if you can find them. Not that the smash up comes without warning; there is a distance signal on your line that generally works, and you have a trace of the Scorpio laziness which lies near the border of your sign and you can lie down and rest without carrying on your work in your dreams. So it generally happens that you last out. You are full of fun and wit, quite resentful, and rapid, sometimes reckless. You are a fluent, eloquent talker, and every word contains an idea. Your executive, mechanical and commercial traits are strong and manifest and you push your schemes to a successful issue. In short, you belong to the class who keep the world moving. The Libra nature is the balance point of the mental zodiac. Strongly marked characteristics of every other sign are found in it, and it is perhaps the most versatile and rich in possibilities of the whole series. A Libra person is an interesting study, but it takes a lively observer to keep up with it. You are pretty apt to excite the wonder and amazement of the world, perhaps the consternation of your friends, for you drive a fast and spirited horse.

Sign of Zodiac ♏ SCORPIO

Begins October 24—Ends November 22

GEM: TOPAZ. COLORS: DARK BLUE AND RED.

October 24, 25, 26, 27, 28, 29.

Occupations: Lawyer, Manager, Jurist, Lecturer, Military Commander, Surgeon.

October 24, 25, 26.

These dates lie under the cusp of Libra and Scorpio, and you unite the dash and vim of Libra with the moody, forceful laziness of Scorpio. You can surmount any obstacle, or balk at a rail fence. You are determined to succeed up to the very point of attainment, when you may suddenly stop and throw the result of all your endeavor overboard. With the faculty of pleasing to an unbounded degree, capable of the extreme of courtesy, your unconventionalism and careless indifference regarding the little amenities of life sometimes render you a most insufferable bore. You are rather envious of the success of others, especially if it in any way interferes with your own. You are jealous, and a look or suggestion of courtesy or approbation directed towards a supposed rival sends you into a rage. You are apt to be suspicious of your mate, and if you don't know where he or she is every moment you sometimes begin to imagine something wrong and work yourself into a frenzy. If you are a woman your jealousy takes in not only your husband, but son-in-law also. You don't give him more than a tongue lashing very often, but you want to kill somebody. If there is any attention or courtesy to be shown, you want all, and it often happens that you drive your husband away in search of the peace he cannot have at home. But if he flatters you, pays you every attention, and pets you all the time, you can be intensely, devotedly sweet and loving. If you are a man, you do not show this trait so much on the surface, but it runs deep. You do not have many friends, but those you have are generally fond of you, for there is something to you. You are not satisfied with the existing order of things, but while that order exists you obey it, and go in for making others do it. (See note No. 5 at end of readings.)

October 27, 28, 29.

Like all Scorpio people, nothing, even the private affairs of others, can be hidden from you, if you desire to know them, and you have boundless capacity for becoming a repository of information and knowledge far beyond any other sign of the Zodiac, but you do not always employ your powers in an absolutely unselfish way. You have the gift of eloquence, not only as a public speaker, but as a conversationalist, and your listeners hang on your words,—which always carry conviction with them,—whether sincere or not,—in absolute helplessness. Like the surf of the ocean, which symbolizes this nature, you carry everything before you, and dash your energy against the solid rock of fact. And unless you learn restraint and hold your lower nature down, you may suffer in more ways than one, and bring suffering and disaster to others. Not that your nature is worse than some other people's, but, like the ocean when lashed by storms, you are terribly intense and ungovernable. And after the storm has passed you absolutely hate yourself.

❧ ❧

October 30, 31; November 1.

Occupations: Doctor, Surgeon, Chemist, Clergyman, Musician, Orator.

October 30, 31; November 1.

You are motherly and kind, even if a man, very sensitive and very easily wounded, but you will not show this except to one you dearly love,—and you can love with the intensity of an angel. Possessed of the faculty of learning and retaining much valuable knowledge, you can also make every one, including yourself, believe that you "know it all." But woe to the unlucky wight who holds up the mirror to your own gaze, or pricks the bubble of your assumption and conceit, for he becomes the object of your rage and hatred, until you learn the value of such a friend, *and you will.* You are your own greatest enemy. Like the great ocean, you also hold in solution a multiplicity of things, but that very fact may render you unpleasant. You will never lack for plenty of enemies, nor for a circle of admiring friends, who, smothered by your unquestioned fascination, may sometimes do you more harm than good.

You are critical and condemnatory to the last degree, but hypersensitive to criticism of yourself. And the sooner you come into a realization of this fact, as well as to a knowledge of the designing traits that permeate this really powerful nature, the sooner will you come to an understanding of the purpose of your creation, and the real meaning of life, and know that you possess, to an unbounded degree, the power that moves the world.

You are subject at times to moods of great depression, which quickly change to corresponding elation. It does not require much to irritate you to a high pitch, nor does it take your rage long to subside when the cause of the irritation ceases to operate. Savage and ungovernable as is your anger, it is fortunate for your associates that it is evanescent, and in your calm and peaceful seasons,—which you should learn to increase in frequency and duration,—you are strongly and lovingly helpful. You are a paradox. Underneath all this surface nature of storm and tempest you have a deep and tender love nature, and you are very, very easily wounded. With all your irritableness you are domestic, and love home and children. You suffer from your peculiarities and intensity, but you have great power of self-control and endurance. It is the little irritations of life that cause the most of your misery. You would meet a grizzly bear and fight it out with him alone and single-handed, and yet run for shelter from the attack of a swarm of flies. You are daring, reckless, magnanimous. Scorpio never tramples on a conquered enemy. Soldier you might be, and in battle annihilate an army, and then bury your victims with all the honors of war. You are a troublesome problem, and source of anxiety to your friends, and a puzzle to yourself. With a deep and intense love nature, you build about yourself a cold, hard, external shell, and few guess how much tenderness lies beneath and within, for you admit few to your inner rooms. Nothing draws you out of yourself like the tender affection of a little loving child. But if your better nature shows itself sometimes, you are very apt to withdraw it, and lie down under the resultant misunderstanding with a sort of morbid, *discontented* enjoyment.

November 2, 3, 4, 5, 6.

Occupations: Surgeon, Lawyer, Physician, Chemist, Orator, Clergyman.

November 2, 3.

You are impulsive, energetic, independent, extreme, and still, at times, the most sad and disheartened being in the world. Perhaps you may think that I am describing, or endeavoring to describe, an impossible, paradoxical character, but I am accurately defining Scorpio. The Scorpion is a creature of fire in the water. This nature is like Gemini, in that it is markedly dual, but the opposing interests do not occupy the throne *at the same* time, as in the case of Gemini. They are too intensely, deadly in earnest. When the scales fall from the eyes of a Scorpio person, they come off to stay. "Gad, a troop shall overcome him, but *he* shall overcome at the last," and Gad is the mystic individual symbol of Scorpio.

You have one strong characteristic which is common to Scorpio people, and that is you are a deep and fearless investigator in the realms of occultism. You plunge into the labyrinth of mystery with absolute fearlessness, but you scare your friends sometimes. In fact, be you doctor, chemist, or theologian (and Scorpio can be this latter), you do not waste any time or effort in surface exploration. In your laboratory work you are going to find out all about the composition and nature of the substance in your hand, even if you get blown up. If a physician you look beyond physical symptoms in your diagnosis. If a theologian you dig deeply into first principles and question conceptions and formulations of faith in a daring way, such as frightens your fellow parsons, but doesn't you. And the result of your investigation you exhibit as fearlessly, quietly assuming that if the denominational creed cannot stand the light of the revelation, so much the worse for the creed. This is all very well, but remember, Scorpio, that while you have a power for good, and a firm grasp on that power, you can also do an immense amount of mischief. Exercise your energy to the utmost in the interest of higher use, and the world will be the better and human life fuller and richer for your having lived in it. But be watchful, and careful how you lower your standard, for when you fall you are apt to take others with you.

November 4, 5, 6.

You are not so hopeful, so enthusiastic as some others of your sign. If you meet with defeat you grow sad, and get inside of yourself, hide yourself, like the scorpion, under a big stone, and throw your sting if anyone moves it. It will not do, my friend. Scorpio needs the sunlight, not gloom, to bask in. You have enough of gloom in your interior nature. The ocean looks bright and beautiful in the sunlight, but dismally dull and gray under a cloudy sky. Kindness excites your gratitude but you get little of it as a rule from others, and none from yourself. Come out into the sunshine. Be more hopeful. If your efforts for the good of others do not meet with appreciation don't relax them, pursue your course and *wait*. GOD *waits*. Hammering is good for you; some metals need it, and it matters not if you are on the anvil if the hand of DIVINE LOVE wields the hammer. GOD wastes no time on useless material, and if HE has you in HIS forge, make up your mind that HE has a use for you—needs you.

❧ ❧

November 7, 8, 9, 10, 11.

Occupations: Musician, Chemist, Philosopher, Lawyer, Jurist.

November 7, 8.

You are of a fiery, persistent, determined nature, but you often get strangely cheated and taken advantage of. You are great at planning and scheming, but not always successful. You have musical ability, but with more of dash and weirdness than method. You despise technique. You get there in your own way, and according to your own ideas, or stay away. You have a deep, intense leading towards the mysterious and occult. You are a deep student of causation, and have the qualifications for a deep and analytic chemist. You enjoy fun, and with all the tragedy in your make-up, you do not want it on the stage. You prefer rollicking comedy. You are very often misunderstood and often receive criticism and blame wrongfully. You rarely get fully paid for what you do, and you are sometimes driven to the exercise of shrewd methods which you do not like, in order to gain half that belongs to you, and for whatever you do, you will receive a larger remuneration if you let the other fellow set the price. That is, if he intends to pay you at all,—and lots of people don't. Fortunately for you, you often have friends who lend a helping hand, for you will not fight for what belongs to you, and in the end you do get your own.

November 9, 10, 11.

As for you, my friend, you always have a fight on hand and generally the antagonist is yourself. You have much to overcome, and generally win the fight, but often in the last round, after you have been thoroughly pounded. You are a great reader, but your taste does not run towards the volatile, frivolous literature of the day. It is the deep, mysterious, occult, that deals with the deeper things of life. Balzac, Paracelsus, Boehme, Corelli, are more to your taste than Mayne Reid or Emma Southworth. Get acquainted with them. You take a deep interest in public affairs, but are rarely found in politics. You have great musical and artistic ability, but sometimes lack confidence in yourself, although you may astonish people by making a sudden and successful dash. This is a somewhat common trait in Scorpio. If you have only seen the scorpion crawl leisurely over a sunny rock, you might be surprised to see how fast he can run. You are secretive, and not apt to pour out your soul to every one. But when one has won your confidence, and, what is far more with you, your love, he is apt to wonder at what lies underneath. Did you ever try to pull a rat out of his hole by the tail? He pulls himself way in and leaves the skin of his tail in your hand. And that is the result when any one tries to force any expression of your ability from you.

❧ ❧

November 12, 13, 14, 15, 16.

Occupations: Musician, Lawyer, Jurist, Chemist, Clergyman.

November 12, 13.

As the sun moves into these degrees, although the general characteristics of Scorpio rule, the more undesirable features of the nature seem modified. They are there certainly, for Scorpio is a most compact, homogeneous mass. But you whose nativities fall in these latter degrees have an easier time with your regenerative process than your comrades who enter the arena when the burden and heat of the day are stronger and heavier. But you have the general characteristics of the nature. You are susceptible to flattery to a large extent. You are magnetic, philosophical, psychic, inventive, and full of fun. You have great self-control, especially if polarized. You have fine mental ability, but a vein of sadness and anxiety runs through your nature. You have a love of travel, want to be on the go all the time, but never quite shake off the ties that bind you to home.

November 14, 15, 16.

You have great self-control. You can stand a large amount of abusive words, and a torrent of undesired and ill-timed advice, and keep absolutely silent. But the donor is likely to get it back. There is a curious animal of the Llama species in the Zoological Garden in London that will eat anything you give him. It is considered very fine fun to feed hand bills and paper wads to him, which he seems to masticate and swallow with much satisfaction. But if you "don't know the critter" you may meet with a surprise, for he will give a sudden gulp and cough and send the whole contents of his stomach all over you. And so you do, friend Scorpio. You take the dose very quietly for a while, but it comes up sooner or later. You are affectionate and kind, make many warm friends, and do not often give intentional offense. Your mental leadings are towards the scientific. You are musical and fond of art in every form. Love to be on the water. You are generally truthful and trustworthy. You have periods of melancholy, but emerge from them without much harm. You would succeed as an inventor, having great originality. You don't follow much in the wake of other people, either in thought or operation. You have a fair degree of pride, love to command, although you like sometimes to have one in authority over you, to take the responsibility of the failures perhaps. This is quite a trait in the Scorpio make-up.

❧ ❧

November 17, 18, 19, 20, 21, 22.

Occupations: A versatile Lawyer, eloquent Preacher, fine Salesman, but poor Collector.

November 17, 18, 19.

You would make a successful merchant though you should have a partner to look after the financial department. Man or woman, you are a good buyer, and have a good idea of what will sell, and you generally sell it. You don't have much dead stock left on hand at the close of the season. You are a fine companion, bright and interesting in conversation. You are affectionate, and love to shine, have the gift of eloquence in a marked degree. You are naturally cheerful, but have your glum spells, generally from your own carelessness.

You are fond of the occult, love the grand in nature, and like to sit by the ocean, especially on a rocky shore, but you enjoy this occupation best alone, for you don't want any one to speak to you then. You meet with losses, through misplaced confidence. Things turn out all right with you in the end, but your life channel takes a somewhat tortuous course.

November 20, 21, 22.

Your traits lead you strongly in the direction of public and political life, and you are not infrequently found in positions of responsibility and trust. Your intentions are pure and good. You are an independent thinker, not apt to follow in any man's lead, and might at times kick out of the party trace. But people would trust you all the same. Unlike those born under the first degrees of Scorpio, you are prompt and reliable, and can be depended on. You know how to keep your own counsel, as all Scorpio people do, and no one can worm your secret from you, except like Delilah, by playing upon your love, and this is true of every Scorpio person, especially if a man.

I have avoided giving or volunteering much advice in the course of these delineations, but shall include a little advice in this closing paragraph. It is—for the woman—to avoid the habit of petty nagging and fault finding, and to control the disposition to demand perpetual flattery and notice from her husband, and for the man to *turn his desires into the higher channels.* As to associates, Virgo people will prove true friends, as they will mercilessly puncture your bubbles of pretense, but in a kindly way, and "faithful are the wounds of a friend."

Sign of Zodiac ♐ SAGITTARIUS

Begins November 23—Ends December 22

GEM: CARBUNCLE. COLORS: INDIGO AND GREEN.

November 23, 24, 25, 26, 27, 28.

Occupations: Soldier, Surgeon, Lawyer, Teacher (vocal), Operatic Singer, Actor.

November 23, 24, 25.

These dates lie under the cusp of Scorpio and Sagittarius. You are positive, fearless, masterful. You were born to command, and you generally do. You are impatient of dictation and interference, and rather blunt and forcible in telling people to get out of your way. Any one who interferes in your work is certain to hear from it in unmistakable language. Fear has no restraint for you, but you may yield from motives of policy. If your tendency is downward you go down like a toboggan, but you stop suddenly when you choose. You are apt to be tyrannical and devoid of feeling. You are a strict disciplinarian and determined to enforce obedience. You expect and desire appreciation, and if your efforts do not meet with such appreciation and the praise to which you consider yourself entitled is not rendered you, you will become morose and moody, and although you will continue to perform your duties with faithfulness and completeness, the performance will be perfunctory. Nothing will make you remiss in this direction, but it will simply be giving a fair quid pro quo. With all your external assumption of indifference, you are deeply sensitive. You are fretful if things do not go your way. Perhaps the fault may lie largely with yourself, for you are in a measure unapproachable, violently opposed to dictation or interference, and do not attract people in a confidential way. You are somewhat suspicious, and have a fair share of Scorpio jealousy.

November 26, 27, 28.

You have a strong will; don't like to acknowledge yourself

in the wrong, or own up to a mistake. You are infallible, like to have your efforts succeed, and bend all your energies to their accomplishment, and insist on the same energetic disposition on the part of those associated with you, who generally happen to be under your direction. But in the division of the spoils, the glory ensuing from a successful issue, you prefer to be the recipient of all the credit, to be divided up according to your own ideas, and the lion's share generally tends in your direction; assuredly so if you have the entire management. Still you do not withhold the praise to which you consider another entitled, although that other generally earns all you give him. Nor are you in the least sparing of your denunciation. You like to command the ship, although you recognize the ability of your crew. You make some intense enemies, and a few friends, who appreciate your unflinching faithfulness and devotion to duty. Even if you consider yourself over-reached, and not justly dealt with, you render all you agree to and sometimes more. Your peck measure holds eight full quarts, and you pile it up, and do not shake what little overflow there may be back into your own barrel, but you are perfectly conscious that you give good measure and take good care that your customer knows it. You are fond of fine clothes, which must be of the best possible material and fashionable cut. You like jewelry, but want no tinsel or paste.

❧ ❧

November 29, 30, December 1, 2, 3.

Occupations: Musician, Artist, Florist.

November 29, 30, December 1.

You are fiery, determined, generally quick to decide and act, but can bide your time. You are a good talker, grand mimic, jovial and a good fellow, with your equals. You are fond of society, sports, games, something of a stickler for established forms, but can adapt yourself to circumstances that don't quite suit you. You are very thorough.

You learn readily, retain what you learn, and might occupy a brilliant position if you did not fret yourself to death, and involve others in the process. *Don't do it.* You are not over-ready to acknowledge yourself mistaken, but when convinced that you are, you make a most thorough and complete acknowledgment of it. You thoroughly understand your own business and have no time nor inclination to interfere with that of any-one else. Your own affairs are quite enough for your own attention, and you do not fancy any interference with or prying into them. Your own mistakes—and you will make them,—are your own affair, and you do not ask any one else to help you carry the results. If you lose money it is your own loss. If you err in judgment you accept the resultant condition and do not ask for sympathy, nor care for criticism. You are combative, quick-tempered, fond of commendation, if you think it deserved, but have little use for servile flattery. You are not in the habit of tendering advice, and prefer to let people pursue their own course and take what comes. You have a tendency toward mysticism, but do not let it stand in the way of your work. You have a plenty of self-confidence.

December 2, 3.

You are persistent, brave, not easily turned aside from your chosen course, quite reserved, and can live much within yourself. Generally quiet, you can be aroused to a high pitch of excitement. Are sometimes hasty in speech and decision, but quick and willing to see your mistake. You have an inflexible love of justice, and would not knowingly wrong any one, but you like to see people get, what you consider their just deserts. While not vindictive or revengeful, you can get entirely through with a person, even a friend, and have no further use for him, and carry your feeling no further in the way of punishment or retaliation. But you make mistakes sometimes in this direction, and turn against a real friend. You are fond of fun if it does not interfere with business. You are rather set in your religious opinions, a devoted churchman, with due regard for externalities and forms. If you are a clergyman you will be likely to be a bishop.

❧ ❧

December 4, 5, 6, 7, 8.

Occupations: Musician, Artist, Merchant, Jeweler.

December 4, 5, 6.

You are energetic, shrewd, capable, somewhat cunning. You want to be in the van, are fond of finery, jewelry, and the best is none too good for you. You have a fondness for animals, a love of nature, and love to cultivate and live among flowers.

There are many things in life that puzzle you. With a sincere and true regard for your friends, you are apt to quarrel with them, often the very best one, for you are impulsive and fiery and sometimes misunderstand others.

You are anxious for the future, cautious in your movements, generally reliable in your friendships, and loyal to your friends. You like good living, and plenty of it. You are slow to make friends, reserved, reticent, rather dogmatic, distant, but you sometimes unbend. You are cautious, in everything, but go it when you are ready. Ingratitude sours and offends you. If you show a kindness you don't want it forgotten. You are obliging generally, but you say "No," and stick to it. As a mother you are rather severe and exacting, enforcing obedience rigidly and positively.

December 7, 8.

You have much native intelligence, keen foresight, amounting almost to a prophetic instinct. What you aim at you hit, and your words go straight to the point. You get angry and say harsh things, but you regret it afterwards. You are sympathetic and kind, and like to be helpful. You are fond of the mysterious and unseen, and may be a fine psychic or clairvoyant. You are faithful and honorable, generally sincere, and want others to be. History and philosophy are your favorite studies, and you have a retentive memory. You are a pleasing speaker and instructive lecturer. You have a quick wit, pleasant sort of sarcasm and can make things that you are disposed to criticise look very ridiculous and at the same time amusing. Humbug stands very little chance with you, and you puncture empty pretense in a most entertaining way.

❧ ❧

December 9, 10, 11, 12, 13.

Occupations: Clergyman, Business Manager, Lecturer, Historian, Salesman.

December 9, 10, 11.

You have much native intelligence, with a faculty almost prophetic. You are direct in your decision and aim. You always hit the mark. You have strong imagination, and are apt sometimes to overstate things. You can be, and are likely to be, a pessimist,—a sort of psychical and mental storm prophet.

The things which threaten calamity are the things that most forcibly impress themselves on your prophetic consciousness. If you pursue the study and practice of psychology, you will be a prophet of evil. This is not said in any offensive sense, for such warnings are of much value, if one is wise enough to take them, and give them a careful and discriminating study. Do not think that I am enlarging upon this matter as a Sagittarius *fault*. The writer has a cherished friend who belongs to this part of Sagittarius, to whom he owes many an escape from serious harm, not only in a spiritual, but also physical way. It is not to be assumed that all of your darker musings will prove actual revealments of inevitable harm, but you can be of great use to those of your friends who know how to appreciate this gift which you possess in a marked degree. The chief occupation of the employees of the light-house department is marking sunken rocks and shoals with beacon and bell buoy. And the writer is strongly impressed with the conviction that the intuitive warnings and suggestions, which seem to be in the power of you of this division of Sagittarius to impart, if you develop this splendid faculty, are worth far more than the meddlesome, incessant nagging of certain other people. Your way is to point out the dangerous reef, and then let the man run on to it or avoid it, as he chooses. *Your* responsibility ends here, and you have a very satisfactory way of giving the desired information, without interfering with the freedom of the individual. But some mentors are determined that one *shall* shape his or her course according to the advice, and insist on bothering the man at the helm, tipping the compass upside down, overhauling the ballast, thereby destroying their usefulness, and becoming nuisances that one must throw overboard to get rid of. The writer has thus enlarged on this great possibility of Sagittarius, because it seems to him that it is a manifestation of a helpful principle that is much neglected. The advice that has to be sought and that comes in the form of suggestions, is after all, to his mind, of more value than that which obtrudes itself. The sign of Sagittarius in the mystic planisphere, is symbolized by Joseph, the revealer of dreams, who whether in prison or viceregent of Egypt, scents the coming danger and *suggests* how to meet it.

December 12, 13.

You are rather proud, self-satisfied, self-confident. You are capable and have a keen and brilliant intellect. Public affairs interest you, and you watch the course of events with an understanding and psychic comprehension that is often prophetic. You are fond of amusement and pleasure and like to have company on your excursions. You are thoughtful of others, and if a day's pleasure trip is on your program, you look up some less favored individual to share it with you. You have rather large ideas in business, and are apt to mount a horse too large for you to straddle, and off you tumble. You can be passionate and excitable, but are generally cool, collected and a desirable companion.

❧ ❧

December 14, 15, 16, 17, 18.

Occupations: Lecturer, Historian, Merchant, Clergyman.

December 14, 15, 16.

You are shrewd and determined, desirous of your own way in everything, still with more regard for the feelings of others than many born in the first degree of this sign. You love your home, but you like to move and find change of scene and environment, but you take your home with you. You lay much stress on outward appearance and have some love of show. You love to study and live in the mysterious, and by this is implied, wherever in these pages the suggestion is found, a desire to become associated with mystic orders like Masonry, and people with a love for the occult and mysterious generally find their way into this fraternity, where they find much to interest them,—"for this well is deep." You are a great reader, and have a retentive memory, and what you read is generally assimilated, and becomes a part of yourself. You give out your information as though it were your own,—and really it is. "For great thoughts belong only and truly to him whose mind can hold them. No matter who first puts them in words, if they come to a soul and fill it, they belong to it,—whether they floated on the voice of others,—or on the wings of silence and the night."

December 17, 18.

Your ideas are rather large and you sometimes undertake more than you can accomplish. Do not "despise the day of small things." Remember that in the problem of the soul's evolution *nothing* is small. Fond of change and want to be always "on the go." You can be very quarrelsome, and bitter in your denunciation of those who stand in your way, or who oppose your desires. You have a certain reserve that makes you somewhat unapproachable. You do not always state the truth accurately,—not intending to prevaricate either. You belong to that class of people who are termed "too previous." You outrun yourself and sometimes things which are only seemings are regarded and represented by you as facts. You are domestic in taste and love home, but there are occasional outbreaks there, for you are excitable. You keep your own affairs to yourself, and are willing that others should do the same. You are just to all, and true to your friends. You have strong religious tendency, and if you are agnostic you do not doubt or deny. You are a firm and valued friend generally.

December 19, 20, 21, 22.

Occupations: Dressmaker, Milliner, Artist, Florist, Designer, Decorator.

December 19, 20.

Perhaps you think that in indicating occupations, only those which bring one into prominence are mentioned. But it is not to be supposed that every man is a general or leader. The great mass carry the saw and hammer, the broom and dust pan. But where there is artistic talent it will crop out even if your home is humble and conditions hold you down to a life of toil,—even *struggle* for bread. The woman will buy a dime's worth of ribbon at a bargain counter, a bunch of discarded flowers of the milliner, and with a few scraps of colored silk that her friend gives her will turn her little 7 by 9 room into a bower of beauty. If there is a square yard of space back of the house she will have a flower bed, and always a bouquet on the table. You know this, Mrs. or Miss Sagittarius, and the desire for things of beauty brings them to you. Your tastes and talents are known and appreciated, and every time you pass by the dwelling of your more well-to-do neighbor, bringing your can of milk and loaf of bread for your frugal supper, she stops you to give you a little bunch of pansies, sweet peas and nasturtiums, which look more charming in the center of your supper table than the profusion of "Jack roses" on the board of the millionaire. And once or twice a week she hands you a little bundle of bright colored bits that she has saved out for you. Yes, and if you are a man, you get a little pot of paint and decorate an old kitchen chair so that it ornaments your modest little parlor, and with a little bundle of excelsior and some old hair which the upholsterer gladly *gives* you, and some chintz, you make an easy chair from an old flour barrel that excites the envy of your richer acquaintance, and he gets you to make one for him. And so if these artistic characteristics standing at the head of each division belong to you,—and they certainly do,—they will blossom out like daisies in a mowing field. And Miss Greenbacks has just been in to get your opinion of the best way to trim her new dress, and left that discarded hat of hers for you to trim over for yourself, Mrs. Sagittarius. She won't know it the next time she sees it. Well, to continue our reading of your character, you love music, art, science, and like to look into the deeper things of life. You are quick, energetic, active, and your work seldom gets ahead of you. Take a little more rest, and more frequent recreation, and save yourself from some of those attacks of nervous headache.

December 21, 22.

You are original, bold, brave, and somewhat politic. You like to please people. Your nature is spiritual. You act more from inward motive than from outward influence and example. You don't do a thing because someone else does, nor believe a thing because someone else tells you so. If you think, or act, you do both from your interior consciousness. You are affectionate, you don't fall in love at first sight, however, but when you settle in this state you are there to stay. You are interested in philanthropic work, are trusty, pure minded, and always reliable, and generally satisfied and contented with things as they go, but sometimes worry and bring on morbid physical conditions, especially indigestion and torpidity of the bowels.

Sign of Zodiac ♑ CAPRICORN

Begins December 23—Ends January 20

GEM: ONYX. COLORS: BLACK AND DARK BLUE.

December 23, 24, 25, 26, 27.

Occupations: Teacher, Elocutionist, Musician, Preacher, Lecturer, Bookkeeper.

December 23, 24, 25.

These degrees lie under the cusp of Sagittarius and Capricorn. Their characteristics have more of sparkle and brightness than those lying farther along in the sign. Born at this time, you are a great thinker, and your thought is broad and comprehensive. It is hard to confine you within dogmatic limits, and you chafe under a collar, until you finally throw it off. If a theologian, you are larger than your creed. You may indeed hold to some form of denominational definition, but your sympathy with humanity is too large for any clothes. You see and recognize the good in others, and any difference in mode of thought does not make the grasp of your hand any the less warm or firm. You are a natural teacher, and win and hold the love of your pupils. If a preacher, the wild freedom of some of your expressions may startle your more conservative auditors, but will not weaken your hold on them, and spite of their conservatism and strenuous regard for articles of faith, they often find themselves convinced that after all you may be right. You have the courage of your convictions, and the full, onward rush of your oratory does not notice the barriers of conventional dogmatism. You may not be a leader or originator of systematic conceptions, but you are a potent factor in shaping them. A brilliant illustration of this fact occupies the pulpit of the Old South Church in Boston, the Rev. Dr. Geo. Gordon.

December 26, 27.

You are a great observer of things, just and kindly in your criticisms, and however dark and discouraging the present condition of society, politics, and the world in general may be, you are certain that it is moving onward toward a glorious consummation. It matters not how bad a condition may be if it is *growing better,* and nothing can shake your faith in the fact that *it is.* To your vision, the sun has touched the lowest point in its zodiacal course, and the next move is for a higher point. And although there may be still a period of storm, and cold and ice, you look for the time when returning summer shall break the seal, and roll the stone from the sepulchre of nature.

There is that in your nature that draws you strongly toward the occult and mysterious, but you do not often give expression to this leading in words. But those who are intimate with you are compelled to admit that some voice from out the unseen counsels you, and some unseen hand guides you.

But your life is no pleasure holiday. You are so bent on pushing the world along and banging yourself against the existing order of things, that you strain and bruise yourself. Then you may feel like letting go, and may sink into a period of dejection, but you do not stay there. When the fatigue and hurt have passed you are up and at it again. In the full play of your activity you find no room nor time for doubt, but like Bunyan's pilgrim you sometimes find yourself a prisoner in the dungeon of "Doubting Castle," in the clutch of the giant "Despair," but the key that frees you is in your own bosom.

Capricorn people are hard to understand, but they are worth all the study one will devote to them. Some of the most successful teachers are found in this sign, and they always win the respect and love of their pupils. They win and hold the love of all their associates in spite of their occasional dark moods. If you are a bookkeeper, your books will be models of accuracy, but all the details are according to your own methods and the most able accountant will find your assistance necessary in understanding them. But everything is beautifully accurate. You are capable, somewhat reckless and headstrong, intellectual. Some people in business, who come into contact with you, get mad at you, especially if their own business ways are uncertain and unreliable. But that does not disturb you. In your home you are kind and affectionate, and your children love you.

December 28, 29, 30, 31.

Occupations: Scientist, Artist, Chemist, Musician, Historian.

December 28, 29.

You are fearless, courageous, strenuous, but with all this, very politic in some ways. You know on which side your bread is buttered, even if you sometimes drop it butter side down. You are not apt to sacrifice a principle to profit or gratification. You are capable, somewhat reckless and headstrong, intellectual, but deeply spiritual. Surface study does not answer for you. You want to go down deep in your investigation of hidden causes, even if you sometimes find yourself in an underground cavern and the candle gone out. You are not much given to operating in a small, confined way. Your desire tends toward public uses. You are convincing, smooth, graceful, but forceful in speech, and with marked penetration. While not secretive, and reserved like your Scorpio comrade, you do not parade your affairs before the public. You make no secret of your aims and intentions, for they are generally of the character that can stand the light. There are no hidden corners into which you sweep your mental rubbish in the attempt to conceal it from sight. If you find it advisable to knock a man down, you do it in the broad daylight. You do not fear to have people know what you think, and you will take great chances when you declare war on public wrong or injustice. You do not carry any concealed weapons.

Still in circles of conservative, narrow minded men, those who fear that their free thought may be crime, and earth have too much light, you are regarded as a dangerous person. But this does not trouble you much. Not being given to the shifting of responsibility, or dodging the consequences of words or actions, you do not notice this coterie of adversaries by even a turn of the head. They only attract your attention when they get on the wagon with you, and then you meet them with a ready, hearty welcome.

December 30, 31.

You are thoughtful, contemplative, close in money matters, calculating, shrewd at a bargain and withal deeply religious. If you are a church member you are likely to be a deacon. You are a constant attendant at the evening meetings during the week. Although you are somewhat narrow in your dogmatism, you sometimes broaden out in your thought in a way that surprises even yourself. You are quick to see the good in others, and if you are in a confidential position in a factory, you often speak a good word for some man who shows talent and ability. You sometimes get taken in, but not often twice by the same man. You have many friends, and you are friendly to all. People rather like to have you around. If you are the head bookkeeper of a large corporation, no clerk shakes in his boots when you come in in the morning, unless he is dishonest or a shirk, in which case he doesn't stay under you a great while. While you can see and censure carelessness or inattention to business, you much prefer to commend and encourage. The affairs of your department generally run smoothly and orderly. You are just and thoughtful in your relations with your subordinates, and do not demand more than is due. When the bell strikes for shutting down you clear the office of every one, and if you think some one is tired and overworked you send him out before closing time, even if you have to finish his work yourself. If you are a well-to-do housewife, your hired girl does not have to fight for her evening off, and you give her an extra one when you can. There are not many strikes in your factory or home, for you are just and regardful of the rights of others, and you concede them. Thorough-going honesty and integrity, and steady application to duty count more with you than flashy brilliancy.

☙ ☙

January 1, 2, 3, 4, 5.

Occupations: Dramatist, Poet, Musician, Teacher, Actor, perhaps Comedian.

January 1, 2.

You have much executive ability and like to be the leader in everything, small or great, though sometimes with much doubt of the absolute success of your undertakings. You have much determination of character, and are determined to carry your point. You are a deep lover of your own family, whether children, or brothers and sisters, and want to make everything smooth and easy for them. You would cut a swath through a neighbor's wheat field to make a short cut for them, and then fight for its possession. You do not trouble about the highway if there is a shorter cut over the fence and through someone's yard. You are sympathetic in your own home, but not diffusive in that way outside. But you are dearly loved by a large circle of friends, in spite of your tendency to abruptness in speech. You are always "breaking out in a new spot," and are quite an interesting problem to your friends. If you are a housekeeper, you have some slack ways. There may not be much dirt in sight, but it can be found in obscure corners. You do not run your broom under the bureau or bed very often, except to sweep the dust out of sight in that direction. You have quite a vein of jollity, and in your lively moods excite much mirth by your peculiar, comical, perhaps unconventional, expressions. Keep your eye on the corners.

January 3, 4, 5.

You have an off hand, jolly way of assuming control, and people often fall in the way of letting you run things for the fun there is in it, and the certainty of having a good time out of it all. You are not dictatorial in the least, but you carry everything your way at home, in a rollicking, good-natured way. You love your children devotedly, and they do you, and you like to have them show it. The children think mother "just too good for anything," especially the girls, and father, when he comes home, does not mind if seven or eight of the children climb over him at once, while baby in her high chair makes vigorous vocal protest because she can't get there too. And you like this strenuous manifestation of affection, if your last clean collar gets mussed during the process, or a button or two comes off. And if both father and mother belong to Capricorn it is apt to be a lively household. The neighbors say "you are a comical crowd but *so noisy*." You are musical and there is apt to be a piano in the house, and if so, it is useless for the neighborhood to go to bed until you and your crowd have turned in for the night. Sometimes, perhaps you are restless, often keeping up an aimless activity that amuses people,—until they get tired of it. You love travelling, even if within circumscribed limits. You have the power of self-control, although you do not always use it. You are a very affectionate parent or child, and unlike most Capricorn people demonstrative of your affection, and like to have others manifest it, if they are very near and dear to you, although your warmest side is turned towards home. You like appreciation and applause, although as a general thing you do not care much what people think of you, so long as you have a tolerable opinion of yourself. In fact, you are a very interesting, enjoyable, companionable character, so long as you live in the upper rooms of your spiritual house. You have a basement and cellar, however,—*keep out of the them.* And to the good things of life, while you enjoy good living it is not an absolute necessity to you. You can have a picnic on a bag of ham sandwiches.

☙ ☙

Jan. 6, 7, 8, 9, 10.

Occupations: Broker, Banker, Lawyer, Clerk, Railway Manager.

January 6, 7.

You possess much mechanical ability, are a good financier, careful and watchful of your interests, affectionate, just, when the exercise of this virtue is not detrimental to your own interests, but Number One stands at the head of the column. You are stubborn, retaliative, have a fondness for giving advice, mysterious in your designs and movements, and capable of low cunning and trickery. With a knowledge and understanding of what is just and right, you do not always choose to live up to this knowledge. You are capable of being intensely selfish and unreliable, and the darker traits of the nature of Saturn—which rules this sign,—are very prominent in these degrees, and under some conditions you will find the weight that holds you down a very heavy one. This is not said in discouragement, but only as a suggestion that you "will not be carried to the skies on flowery beds of ease"; you have a latent power that will aid in overcoming your downward or selfish tendencies, and with your really keen, discerning mind you *know,* without being told, the things that belong to your peace.

January 8, 9, 10.

Your life is pretty certain to be a continual fight against worldly tendencies unless you choose to patch up a truce with them and let them have the rule and sway, which you are not always willing to do. But you get many a discouraging and disheartening upset. You are methodical, careful and look ahead, but you are like the "down east" pilot, who was taking a schooner up Penobscot Bay. He was telling the captain that "he knew the position of every rock on the coast," and then, as the craft ran up high and dry on a submerged ledge, said, "and that's one of them." With the purest and best of intentions, and a general knowledge of cause and effect, you are continually striking some snag. Perhaps you depend too much on your *knowledge* of chart and compass, and do not keep your *eye* on them. You know that the dust lies on your floor, and you go at it with broom and brush without sprinkling first, and get smothered in the dust you raise. With your natural tendency to doubt and distrust why do you monkey with doubt? Turn your thought current the other way;—you know the pleasure of living for others,—try it in practice, and remember that "the love that kills is the love of self, and the hand that smites thee is *thine own.*"

❧ ❧

January 11, 12, 13, 14, 15.

Occupations: Trader, Shop-keeper, Speculator, Contractor, Inventor, Detective, Prison Warden.

January 11, 12.

The faculty of invention is strongly evidenced in these degrees. Your mind is generally well-balanced, and your judgment accurate, careful, sound, especially on the side of self-interest. Money making is your principal aim in life, and you pursue your object in a far-sighted, determined, undeviating way. And while you may, and often do, have the reputation of being close, sharp, shrewd in your dealings, taking care to have the beam of the scales tip in your favor, you generally manage to hold on to your customers. People growl about you behind your back, but continue to patronize you. For with a somewhat quick temper and caustic tongue you have the faculty of controlling both, and making friends. On the whole people like you. You are quite sympathetic with suffering, but you are not given to showing it, and what good you do in your way you do not make a parade of. You are very apt to understand your business, thoroughly, and know where the best goods are to be found at the lowest rates. You are a shrewd buyer, and equally shrewd seller, and people of your stripe do not often make their appearance in the bankruptcy court. You do not take kindly to partnerships, preferring to go it alone, and keep your wallet or checkbook in your own pocket. You show much judgment and shrewdness in your selection of assistants, and do not often get victimized by employees. You know how to smooth over little irritations that sometimes spring up between trader and customer. On the whole you seem to be able to make friends and keep them. Sometimes it may be that you do not find time to be over neat, and if premises are cramped, your place may show some confusion. You are devoted to your family, and think your children are about right, and you are very patient with them and apt to let them have their own way. You have much physical endurance, and insensibility to pain, and will not stay away from business, nor let your needle rust in the cushion because you have a toothache. Worldly affairs are your principal consideration, and Sunday chiefly valuable as a relaxation from the ordinary grind of business. You are fond of sports and recreation, but will not let them interfere with business. But your children generally have a good time, and you let them have opportunity to enjoy life if there is not much expenditure of money connected with it. Your marriage relations are not always the happiest in the world, as worldly interest is often a large factor in the calculation.

January 13, 14, 15.

These natures are apt to be shrewd, cunning, and sometimes a little foxy, as they are deep and secret planners, mysterious and scientific. They are military in their administration and discipline, and worshippers at the shrine of cold, rigid justice. You who are born at this time can suffer, and see others suffer through their own acts. Nothing in the way of calamity seems to disturb you. If you have religious tendencies they are Calvinistic. You bow only to DIVINE SOVEREIGNTY. You are not in the least weak or sentimental, and you often make an unhappy marriage. As a business man you can drive your engine over any track, even if the sleepers or ties belong to others. You believe in trusts as the correct thing, provided you are on the wagon. You may show a lavish apparent generosity, but what you give, you grind out of others, and you look out that your benefactions work toward your own aggrandizement. Well, you have your use. Stone makes a good underpinning for a house, but a very undesirable bed, and you are likely to make a stone bed for yourself. Turn about then, and get out into the sunshine and *melt*. Like ore there is much that is valuable in your composition, but it requires pulverizing and the action of fire to separate the real metal. Go inside yourself with the light of truth and examine your ruling loves and motives, and consider. The wise man rules his stars; do thou likewise.

❧ ❧

January 16, 17, 18, 19, 20.

Occupations: Artist, Decorator, Jurist, Lawyer, Clergyman, Journalist, Banker, Merchant.

January 16, 17.

Under these degrees the gloom of Capricorn seems rapidly to fade and dissolve. The dawn merges quickly into day. You have marked executive talent; are positive, honest, earnest. Your higher spiritual faculties are capable of phenomenal development. You have an unbounded ability to see through everything,—men and things. You have an artistic poetic nature, are loving and true. You are a ready and sound reasoner, have strong convictions, stubborn and somewhat dogmatic, but sincere and honest. No one can reasonably doubt your sincerity. Sudden and strange experiences come into your life, but they are generally uplifting. Your strong trait is an inflexible love of justice. You move slowly in new undertakings, but you make few mistakes, and your native acumen and the confidence you inspire, are very certain to place you at the head of everything into which you enter. If you are not the throne, you are the power behind the throne. You do not belong to the class who become defaulters or breakers of trust. You are fond of the mysterious and have a deep spiritual nature. You do not fling money away lavishly, and although you love display, have pride of position and much ambition. You will not sacrifice principle to gain, either. Tinsel or plate are not in your make up. You may have enemies but they are such through jealousy, envy, or fear of your power of discerning sham and dishonesty. You may be charitable in your judgment of human weakness, and tolerant of a certain amount of moral lacking, but you will never place those who manifest these traits in positions of responsibility or trust. In your administration of your own or public affairs you take no chances.

January 18, 19, 20.

Great executive ability, acute reasoning powers, fine intellect. You have a judicial mind, keen and discriminating. You can command, and put much force into your projects. You are cautious in expenditure, and make every cent procure a cent's worth. You watch the grocer's scales,—perhaps keep a set at home. Your opinions are tenaciously held, and convictions firm and fixed. You have a good business head, are slow in conclusions, but generally correct. You are a clear and powerful writer. Responsibility does not weigh very heavily on you. You are a convincing speaker, a powerful orator. You are poetic and artistic, inclined to spirituality and mysticism. At home you are kind and affectionate. In ways unsuspected even by yourself you do an immense amount of good. Your office seems to be to clear the mental and intellectual atmosphere, and in the mercantile world you are the man who allays a money panic. You are a good man for a board of arbitration, capable of taking a comprehensive view of both interests in dispute. You don't pull your physical system to pieces through undue haste or excitement. You keep your head clear, and your powder dry. You are ready for any emergency and know how to meet it. People generally may not love you, but they trust you, and it is not often that you betray their confidence. They stick to you and follow your lead, and repose confidence in you, even if they do not always agree with your opinions. People of your stamp are the balance wheels of society and the general frame work of civilization, and though politicians may attack you on the stump, the people vote for you at the polls.

Sign of Zodiac ♒ AQUARIUS

Begins January 21—Ends February 19

GEM: BLUE SAPPHIRE. COLORS: LIGHT BLUE AND YELLOW.

January 21, 22, 23, 24, 25.

Occupations: Broker, Insurance Agent, General Business.

January 21, 22.

Born on these dates, you come under the cusp of Capricorn and Aquarius. You are cool, cautious in some degree, active, restless. Generally truthful, though you lack frankness. The average Aquarius individual will tell the truth,—the whole truth in time,—but will generally tell it on the installment plan,—with a certain amount of fiction and economy of important fact mixed up with each installment. You may be cute and sly, especially if you are involved in, or promoting some questionable project. You paint your own side of the question a vividly pronounced rose color. You are an adept at worming out of a scrape, sometimes to the great amusement of one who watches you with eyes wide open. You do not always let one know what you are driving at until you have worked yourself into his or her confidence, and then you let the whole intention or business out,—but then only in sections, while your friend looks on highly entertained with the performance. With a certain faculty for concealing things, you are often very transparent. You fit easily and gracefully into any condition providing there is not too much privation connected with it, in which event you as easily and gracefully glide out of it, and forget that you were ever there. You have a sort of piquant good-nature which makes it the easiest matter in the world for you to make voluminous promises, and a still easier matter to break them, which you do with the most charming naivete, which might be annoying if any one knowing you put much confidence in your word. You don't do this through any base motive. Your shortcomings and peccadillos do not wear a somber hue—at least not often,—but you can be very crooked and are apt to be tricky, though not wishing for a moment to do any one any harm. But you are almost universally liked. You are very generous by spells. You are sometimes original in idea, and you have fits of mulish stubbornness. (Please notice that these remarks are addressed to Aquarius people in general. They apply to the whole sign.)

January 23, 24, 25.

You have a mathematical mind, inventive in excuses and reasons, and are delightfully and amusingly shrewd and cute. It is fun to watch your antics. You sometimes scheme to carry out your designs but you very often spread the net in sight of the bird. You will doubtless make money some way, and have a good amount of intelligence, but you are sometimes slovenly. You gain much light on things of life, but you pay high for it. You are not enthusiastic, rather cool than otherwise. You don't always work openly. You are fond of mysticism. You find many obstacles in life, but generally get over or around them. You have religious tendencies, somewhat shifting, but you are generally loyal to your friends, although you sometimes neglect them. With the grandest possibilities in the world, you scatter your forces without measure. It is the most difficult thing possible for you to sit down calmly and quietly and pull yourself together, but under no other regime can you become anything or accomplish anything. Still you have got to enter on this course of practice with a will and for a deep, earnest purpose, or you will grow stagnant. Reuben mystically stands for this sign. "Bubbling over like water have not thou prominence," were the last words of Jacob to his first born, while at the same time admitting that the principle represented by this man was the beginning of everything that makes the human soul noble and great. Nearly every writer on these subjects gives the stereotyped advice to Aquarius, "Wake Up!" The best advice we can give is, "Don't go to sleep!" You are apt sometimes to mope about, lamenting your inability to accomplish half what is wrought out by those with far less natural ability than you possess. The fault is your own. Your boiler is as full of holes as a colander, and the force you generate wastes out through the punctures. Get yourself to work and stop the leaks, if you would know the latent power within your soul.

January 26, 27, 28, 29, 30.

Occupations: Artist, Musician, Mental Healer, Psychometrist, Superintendent or Matron of Insane Retreat.

January 26, 27.

You are conscientious, have good reasoning powers and much native shrewdness. You take hold of a thing at the start, and pull with much vigor, but you soon get tired if the vehicle does not move fast enough or the others in the harness do not seem to do their share of pulling. You depend too much on others, not sensing your own power to accomplish. Difficulties that are only seeming loom up before you like real obstacles, and you are apt to think a fog bank a rocky headland. You need to get up close to things that oppose you and push them away or push through them. Do not be too ready to doubt your ability to succeed, but *concentrate* your splendid energies, and overcome.

You are ambitious in the higher direction, have intense desire to attain a high and noble and honorable position, but grudge the expenditure of effort necessary to reach your ideal position, while all the time you "waste on trifling cares" more than enough energy to carry you there. The poet must have had you before his mental vision when he sang:

"Know, my soul! thy full salvation;
Rise o'er doubt, and fear, and care."

January 28, 29, 30.

You have an idealistic, poetic, artistic nature. Great achievements are ever before your eyes and beckon you on, but you let them seem distant and beyond your possibility. *They are not.* Nothing is out of your reach if you will keep quiet and grow. Physically,—planetary conditions favoring—Aquarius is tall, commanding in stature. Spiritually he is a giant. You are lacking in staying qualities; in enthusiastic endurance. You are faithful, loving, loyal. If a woman you are a true, devoted wife and mother. You need children in your home. You love the society of congenial friends. You have great psychic power, and rely largely on intuition and inward promptings; in fact sometimes to such an extent that some very matter-of-fact people may consider you subject to hallucinations. Don't pay any attention to these earth worms. They mean well perhaps, but "they don't know."

You have an intense desire, an irrepressible longing to know the why and wherefore of everything, and this characteristic may sometimes lead you where you have no right to be. You are fond of being socially entertained but prefer to entertain others. Your latch string is always out.

❧ ❧

January 31, February 1, 2, 3, 4.

Occupations: Preacher, Teacher, Mental Healer, Musician, Scientist, Natural Philosopher.

January 31, February 1.

There is one characteristic of Aquarius, common in greater or less degree to the whole sign, but markedly prominent from this point on to nearly the end, and that is, the marvelous power of your eye. If you practice concentration and focalization of your powers, you can transfix a person with a look. If your antagonist in argument allows you to fix his gaze on you and you focalize your energy in your own eye, he is "a goner" at once. He will forget what he was talking about. Aquarius women possess this power equally with the men, with this advantage, that they are generally physically beautiful. Do not mistake my meaning. The Aquarius woman shows none of the snaky fascination, behind which lust and unholy desire burn and flash, and snap. It soothes, calms, quiets, subdues excitement. Mysterious and unexplainable as is your power of fascination, it does not Cleopatra-like, awake the devil that slumbers or lurks in every unregenerate man. You do not awaken and draw about yourself the evil sphere of others. You have a phenomenal power over the insane and can quiet the fiercest demoniac. I mean, *if you have centered your powers—in the breast.* (Pardon the occult flavor of this suggestion.) But the writer recalls the experience of a friend,—a delicate appearing Aquarius woman, who a few years ago studied hypnotism. Acting on the suggestion of some friends she visited one of the largest insane asylums of this state,—Massachusetts,—the superintendent of which had little faith in any controlling force other than chains and locks. This woman in company with the superintendent visited nearly all the wards, and astonished him by her power over the milder patients. Finally she visited the department of the violent male patients, and entered the cell of the most violent of all, which was more than any attendant dared to do. The maniac glared at her like a wild beast, but quickly yielded to the power of her gaze, and squatting down on the floor allowed her to gently smooth his hair and stroke his beard. This is the power that the well-centered Aquarius person possesses. There is nothing that can withstand it, if grounded in Love. "And the Lord turned and looked on Peter," and the demon of cowardice went out of him for once and for all. But this is a digression. You have a vein of sceptical materialism to contend with. You want cold, solid, material fact, before you believe. You want to measure the height of Divine Wisdom with your wooden yard stick, and sound the depth of Divine Love with your leaden plummet. You cannot accomplish this, my Aquarius friend, but remember that you have a set of weights and measures within your own soul that will carry you far in this direction, if happily for you, you find it. You make up your mind hastily, but frequently change it on second thought. Early instruction and ideas infused in early days always sway you through life and your thought often comes back to the old home, if only for a visit. You have a vein of scepticism and although you listen to the parson while in the church, you begin to question before you get off the front steps. You are, if a woman, very motherly, (*this is not a trait of the Aquarius man*), and dearly love your family, although it will not be a large one, if you have your way. You are as a general rule hospitable and entertaining, and very fond of animal pets,—especially cats.

February 2, 3, 4.

Critical, opinionated, proud, showy, but tolerably capable of backing up your pretensions with real ability, artistic, musical, stubborn, you can talk up a project and lead people to invest in it. For a promoter of a mining scheme an Aquarius man,—or woman, as to that,—will sell stock certificates faster than they can be printed, and they float many wildcat schemes, believing in them themselves for a time. You have a fine talent for decorating, either your home, yourself or your scheme. You have a habit of getting much at little expenditure, but you get a high price for what you sell. Still you sometimes act very generously toward a friend, especially if that friend has done much for you in any way, but your generosity doesn't empty your pocket. Under favorable conditions you could develop psychic and mystic powers, but you can't keep still long enough. You drop everything if some one puts his head in the door and cries out, "Job lots."

❧ ❧

February 5, 6, 7, 8, 9.

Occupations: Artist, Musician, Poet, Educator, Scientist, Architect.

You are not always practical in your notions. You are a fairly good financier, but rather given to "kite-flying." Your safety lies in your economical tendency. You will not risk anything when there is a chance or probability of losing. You do not often come into a scheme "on the ground floor." You rather wait until the thing becomes an assured success, and then you go in to win. You are not enough of a martyr to enter into a movement, no matter how worthy or philanthropic, when the spectre of possible persecution stands at the door. You go home after something which you have forgotten, or suddenly remember an engagement, which in five minutes you have again forgotten because, while you are on your way to keep it, some friend asks you to take a ride in his carriage. You remember it the next day, and apologize, and are generally forgiven your remissness.

But sometimes you rush into an affair without thought or reason, and sit down and count the cost after the bill comes in, and this is the way you manage sometimes to sit down in a bed of nettles, and it hurts. Still you have fragments of a conscience lying around somewhere, although the bits and pieces don't often get put together for long at a time. You are proud, fond of dress, not much of a home body. You like to be, if a woman, at your social or woman's club, where you can meet congenial associates and shine, but your tastes are scientific and refined, and you don't care for the ordinary small talk of the ordinary social gathering. One would most likely find you in the afternoon at the lecture room of the Metaphysical club, where you are an interested and interesting personality, and in the evening at some scientific lecture. And you make frequent visits to the mothers' association, giving your ideas of the rearing and management of children, which you know lots about, not being likely to be the owner of any yourself. But it is pleasant to hear you expound, and you believe in your ideas and—well, you are a very pleasant sort of person to have around.

February 7, 8, 9.

Good reasoner, fine, active mind, but somewhat impractical, you are sly—sometimes tricky. You enter into large operations, requiring much thought, without using much calculation, and make a mess of it, suffering much disappointment. You begin to build without being able to finish. Your undertakings are like many churches that start a pretentious meeting house and get the basement roofed over, and then worship in the basement for a generation, while the unfinished edifice stands as an eye sore on some conspicuous corner. You lay the under-pinning of a grand house but only complete the ell. Your failures result from lack of forethought. You are artistic, musical, and have refined tastes and high ideals, but you are a long time "getting there."

☘ ☘

February 10, 11, 12, 13, 14.

Occupations: Artist, Marine Architect, Carver, Sculptor, Lawyer, Musician.

February 10, 11, 12.

You are affectionate, tolerably truthful—when it pays to be—conscientious in a degree, rather sly, can be affable and courteous,—if not too much trouble, and very lovable at times. But you have a strong vein of selfishness, that takes in the direction of self-gratification, and you are very domineering. There is no way equal to your way, and you severely denounce the failure and mistakes of others, particularly if they have defeated your desire to have *your* way, by having the thing done *their* way. You never make any mistakes. Oh, no! If your schemes turn out disastrously, or your plans miscarry, it is because someone else has interfered and upset things. You are very stubborn and willful at times. You are strongly attached to your home—at meal times particularly, and like to sleep in your own bed, but you do find it pleasant sometimes to go visiting, especially if you are boss of the expedition and you are left to arrange the fun to your own liking. You are given to adopting the wet blanket treatment for any new project not of your own originating, and have an air of mysteriousness hanging about your schemes, whether of business or pleasure. But people find out generally, and from yourself, too,—what you have been up to. You are sceptical and materialistic to some extent, although you yield faith in time, if you are let alone. Taken all in all, you are rather an interesting character, with grand possibilities that will materialize sometime. You have a great deal of latent talent which you use principally for yourself. What you are compelled to do for others you do with many a grunt and groan, but you work like a car horse for your own fun and enjoyment. Most that you accomplish is through the pushing of friends, for your own efforts at developing your powers are spasmodic and intermittent.

February 13, 14.

You have an intuitive nature, and generally see things in a clear light. Whether you follow that light is a question, for you are a dear lover of ease, except when effort leads to enjoyment and self-gratification. You are inclined to find fault and domineer. You are attached to home and kin, and show strong attachment and much love if it is drawn out of you. You argue every inch of the ground, and continue to argue against doing what you don't want to do, but are compelled to do. And after it is done, and you are all tired out, you go on a long tramp in search of sport or enjoyment and never think of being tired. You come home from your work all used up, and after supper go to the theatre and don't get home until midnight. But spite of all this you are the pet of the household, especially if you are the last baby with a long gap between you and the rest of the family. Perhaps this fact gives undue development to your more selfish traits, but they are not the whole of you. You have much in you that is lovable, and bright, and interesting. Animals like you, particularly the family cat, and you could be ill spared from the family circle.

❧ ❧

February 15, 16, 17, 18, 19.

Occupations: Inventor, Mechanic, Machinist, Musician.

February 15, 16.

The nearness of these degrees to Pisces seems to soften and mellow the flighty nature of Aquarius while the backward working of the Pisces energy gives more activity in a practical way to the sign to which the Sun is speaking his farewell. There is an increased regard for truth and genuine goodness, which seems to flow downward from the ideal plane to the practical. You are faithful and earnest in every calling, mysteriously and strangely nervous, very psychic, and might become an adept in occultism. You see the beautiful side of everything because you will not look at the reverse side. You are quick in thought but deliberate in action. You are anxious, fearful. You have fine artistic tastes, but do not see much use about them, unless you can make them pay. And then you value them. You are a lover of home and kindred, and not happy if long away from them. You are often the favorite and pet of the family, a condition that you are not slow to take advantage of and turn to your own profit. But on the whole you are loved by all, and worthy of the wealth of affection lavished upon you. You are very affectionate, tender, thoroughly good, and don't give any one much reason to worry about you. You do the best you can, and leave it there. You are fond of reading, not over enthusiastic, intellectual but very easily disappointed. You get sad and mournful over your disappointments, but not moody nor sour, and therefore receive much sympathy from others, especially the family.

February 17, 18, 19.

Just and conscientious, intuitive, beautiful, psychic, you are a general favorite both in and out of the house. You have a well balanced mind, with strong artistic tastes, and fond of science. You have an eye for beauty,—ugliness repels you, and you shut your eyes to it. Anything in the line of ornament that is grotesque or hideous has no charm for you. You don't like deformity. You start slow, but move steadily, and do not go to sleep over your work. You know how to turn your artistic tastes and powers to profit. You are a great home lover and fond of your kindred. They like to have you at home and there is a void in the circle when you are away. There is nothing of the spendthrift about you. You anxiously look out for the rainy day. You are a fine psychic, and read the minds of others with ease and accuracy. You are not suspicious but you quickly sense any insincerity or deceit in others, and steer clear of such dispositions. You are not always satisfied with conditions or surroundings, but you don't mope over your dissatisfaction. Your criticisms are direct and pointed but most kindly. Altogether you have a very beautiful nature with few or no angularities.

Sign of Zodiac ♓ PISCES

Begins February 20—Ends March 21

GEM: CHRYSOLITE. COLOR: PURE WHITE.

February 22, 23, 24.

Occupations: Artisan, Mechanic, Musician, Physician, Art Critic, Lecturer, Philanthropist.

February 20, 21.

These dates lie under the cusp of Aquarius and Pisces. Your characteristics are faithful devotion to duty, careful attention to business, and loyal regard for the interests of your employer. You do not skimp nor shirk performance of duty or contract, but rather give more than you are expected to. In social affairs, however, you are good naturedly careless. You make an engagement to please some one, but unless there is some strong attraction of love or deep friendship, when the time arrives you are not there. But if a job connected with your occupation is to be completed, you are on the spot, and if its completion involves overtime, that does not count, even if you get no extra remuneration for it, and the superintendent can go home, well assured that your work will be completed before you leave. But this sort of thing may have an end, for you have spells when you evince a stubborn obstinacy that is amazing, and you may rebel and "throw up the job." Somehow you seem to be able to work under closely drawn and exacting rules and regulations, for a time, without exhibiting the least impatience, when suddenly the traces break and away you go, leaving wagon and driver in the lurch. However, this trait is your protection in a way, for you stand much petty injustice and overloading, and get cheated out of your just due by those who will take advantage of good natured, patient endurance. Then you give a sudden kick, and get out, hardly stopping to pick up your tools.

The foregoing delineation describes the entire basic foundation of the Pisces nature.

February 22, 23, 24.

You are very sweet and lovely, spite of your liability to fret and worry your life out over trifles, and you always win the love and tender regard of others, for you have a deep love nature yourself, and are noble, self-sacrificing, and generous in the extreme. You do not always yield at once to a call or request, —you may for a moment refuse point blank. But you are the son who, when told to go work in the vineyard, refused, "but afterward repented, and went." It is not like you to accept a duty and neglect it.

Generally honest and sincere, you may be very unreliable and inexact in statement. Pisces people under some conditions are terrible prevaricators. They will stick to a lie most persistently. This is the trait, however, more marked in the Pisces *child, for the habit is very largely dropped as they grow older.* But there is nothing malicious about this trait in any of you. You do not tell ugly stories about others. Your prevarication relates to your own affairs. If mother catches you at the jam pot in the store room, you vehemently protest that you were looking for the tacknails. And the very comicality of your innocent claim makes mother laugh, and you don't get spanked. And this is the way you go through life. But you are generally so sweetly good-natured, and have such an innocent way that you are a universal pet.

❧ ❧

February 25, 26, 27, 28, 29.

Occupations: Magnetic Healer, Metaphysician, Psychometrist, Clerk.

February 25, 26.

You are cautious and careful, when not under excitement, and restless. You are fond of society, even a swallow-tailed coat hangs lightly and comfortably on you. Conventionality does not disturb you very much, for if its demands crowd you, you quietly push them over. But you are so absolutely good natured about it that no one takes any offense. You are very "slow to wrath," but sometimes you get into a towering rage,— only for a moment. If you are in a hurry to get into bed, you will tear a refractory shoe-lacing into bits, well aware that you cannot find a new one the next morning within ten miles. But the next morning you sit patiently down and tie the bits together and somehow manage to make it do for a time. You are strongly drawn towards the occult and mysterious, and study its teachings with deep interest. Nothing in statement or theory along this line frightens you much. You do not run away from a shadow, but rather incline to see what causes it. You are not apt to make a parade of what you know in this line, but nothing can disturb your belief in what you know.

Not naturally secretive, you keep all important business whether your own or entrusted to your custody, under lock and key, and the key in your pocket.

February 27, 28, 29.

You are a student and deep reader, and your taste in this line runs to the scientific and philosophical. You have a vivid imagination and strong hope. You are fairly intellectual and a fluent, rapid talker. You venture much in a speculative way, but don't often lose it. If you do, it doesn't kill you, for you feel certain of making it up on the next deal. You are quiet and very obliterative; if you are reading an interesting book no one knows that you are in the house, and if you are disturbed at these times you are off like a rabbit for a new squatting place. You are a nice sort of fellow, or, if a woman, sweet, lovable, and kittenish. You are intensely fond of water sports, especially yachting. In fact, you do not care so much for steamboat travel. You like to have your own hand on the tiller, and meet the varying moods of wind and tide, and feel that you can make them serve you. (See note 8 at end of readings.)

❧ ❧

March 1, 2, 3, 4, 5.

Occupations: Manager, Superintendent, Overseer, Teacher.

March 1, 2.

You are possessed of will and reasoning power in a greater measure than most Pisces people, and have more faith and confidence in your power to do things, and a more dogged persistence in carrying your undertakings to a successful end, than those born under the earlier degrees of Pisces. You know how to apply the lessons of experience, and delays and apparent defeat do not drive you back. If you cannot tunnel through the mountain, you lay your track around it, always looking towards the end in view. In fact the middle and last degrees of Pisces show stronger and more positive characteristics. You know how to hold your tongue, and if you feel the need of a confidant you know how to make a wise choice of one. Your confidence is not often misplaced. You make friends but do not always retain their friendship, and you are at times much dissatisfied, and become morose and faultfinding. You are close in money matters, somewhat apprehensive of the approach of a rainy day, but at times reckless, though seldom dishonest. You pay your bills to the last cent, but when that is gone, your creditor can—wait. You are fond of finery, want *good* things if you can get them. You like a full course dinner but you can dine on a doughnut, if that is all there is in the house, and say nothing,—not even ask a blessing on the meal. You plan well, are rather stubborn, true and loyal to your friends, and spiteful and bitter towards your enemies, although you would not enjoy doing them any serious harm. As a weapon of vengeance you prefer a cow hide to a dagger, or a stone to a bullet. All things considered, you are generally reliable, worthy of confidence, and not given to making failures. And it would not be surprising to find you a leader of men, for you have much tact, and an honest, good natured, dogged honesty and determination that give people confidence in you. You are intensely fond of sports, hunting and fishing.

March 3, 4, 5.

You have a strong, clear mind, and great abilities. You are cautious, careful, far from reckless, and if a financier or public official, you can steer between rocks that a more careless man would run on to. You are musical, poetic, forcefully eloquent, not at all satisfied with the existing order of things. You are very true and faithful to one whom you like, but are capable of strong enmity. You are apt to hold a high and responsible position, and you generally steer clear of complications, but if you get into a snare you cut the strings without stopping to untie them. You have a fashion of meaning what you say, and saying what you mean, and when people know you, they do not fool with you much. You may give one bark before you bite, but not more than one. You are a devotee of sport and recreation, and often found on the water. You do not make many close friendships, but you are reliable and worthy of the confidence that people generally repose in you.

March 6, 7, 8, 9, 10.

Occupations: Artist, Builder, Writer, Musician, Clergyman.

March 6, 7.

You have much executive ability, and a keen, active mind. You see the relation of things to each other, and know where each individual part belongs and will best fit. You show good judgment in your adaptation of means to the end, and will not harness a bull and a mule to the same plough. You have a fair measure of self-reliance and while you may seek advice it does not follow that you will always adopt the resultant suggestion. You like to verify your conclusions, but do not often change them. You demand a *reason* for everything. And this suggests a certain fruitful cause of unhappiness, for Pisces is apt to be strongly drawn towards its most complete antithesis, and that is Libra. And if you want to get into a factory where all the shafting is out of line, and the squeak of every bearing can be heard a mile away, even though it runs in a cupful of oil, just visit a home where one of the partners belongs in Pisces and the other in Libra. Pisces continually and persistently demands a reason for every thought and act, and Libra as persistently and positively refuses it. Let this suggestion pass for what it may be worth. But if you, my Pisces friend, contemplate a matrimonial venture in connection with a Libra individual, this fact may well "give you pause." Water and oil are both fluids but they do not mix. Nothing will blend them but a caustic alkali, and the resultant substance is that nauseating compound—soap—and that is what your progeny will be, if you are so unfortunate as to burden the world with any. Much more might be said along this line, but might not comport with the general design of this book. If you wish to verify the accuracy of this theory instances lie thickly around you. Study them, but hold your tongue.

March 8, 9, 10.

You have an active mind, much shrewd tact, with a general faculty for keeping out of trouble. You are honest, genuine and frank. If a clergyman, you are apt to have socialistic leanings, and be severe in your arraignment of wrong and tyranny. Not many rich men will be found in your congregation. You don't lay much stress on form, ritual, or even dogma. But you have your convictions and you hold them tenaciously, though not offensively. You do not always weigh your words when you attack injustice and wrong. Your psychic nature is so strong, and your intuitive nature so keen, that you often speak with an authority that startles the stickler for dogma and formulated creed. You are progressive, often found on the unpopular side, and have the courage of your convictions. You are very hopeful, broad in your sympathies, and a friend to humanity. With you there is neither Jew nor Gentile, and your ideas and aims tend towards universal brotherhood and equal rights.

❧ ❧

March 11, 12, 13, 14, 15.

Occupations: Musician, Poet, Scientist, Physician, Woodworker, Machinist.

March 11, 12.

You have good business ability, application, and are not in the least lazy. You are a student of science and philosophy. You have a habit of doing what you want to and doing it well. You are fond of home, but exceedingly sensitive to conditions, particularly if inharmonious. You can get very angry if irritated, but are generally good natured. You like fun, and can stand a great deal of rough horse play before you "holler," and your howl is generally an explosion of laughter. Your laugh is infectious, and your rollicking good nature communicates itself to others. You do much in your way, but often get little in return. You are somewhat impractical. People get a great deal out of you, but often give you little in return, though this does not affect you very seriously. You have many friends, who like to be with you on your pleasure excursions. You are often found on the water, and are fond of camping out.

March 13, 14, 15.

You are always sure to be about something when awake if only reading. You do not like an enforced vacation, and although you may sometimes kick over the traces and throw up a job, you at once go on the hunt for another, and in the interim find something to employ your talents. You are not in the least lazy, but after exhausting your energy—as you sometimes do—you can sleep away a day and a night without turning over. You have the faculty of making friends and keeping them and are not much given to demanding any especial attention. You may or may not get your share of what is brought in, but this does not signify much to you. Unlike your Aries brother, who wants to put his teeth into everything eatable that comes into the house, you wait until your share is offered you, and if it is not offered, you do not break your heart about it. Perhaps it is this very trait in your make-up that makes nearly every one careful that you do get your share, for as a general rule you are somewhat of a household pet. You are not overenthusiastic in any direction, but in the way of recreation you get a fair measure of enjoyment, in a quiet way, out of everything.

❧ ❧

March 16, 17, 18, 19, 20, 21.

Occupations: Upholsterer, Decorator, Bookkeeper, Machinist, Clerk.

March 16, 17, 18.

You have good general business ability, and can keep the general run of details, and an accurate account of expenses and receipts. You are faithful to your employer, bear considerable crowding of work and general conditions, and have a sort of happy-go-lucky nature. Somehow you have an idea that everything will turn out all right if you do all you can, and it does generally, even though planetary conditions and influences keep your life down to a perpetual grind. You are somewhat domineering and are dictatorial and harsh with your children, and although you enforce their obedience,—when under your eye,—you seldom gain their confidence or love until the fermentative stage is past,—and that generally lasts until the later years. The better and softer traits of your nature reveal themselves *then,* especially if the grind and wear of life have been in a measure removed. You are impractical in a degree, and often find it necessary to follow the guidance of another. You are very grateful for any kindness shown you or yours, but do not demand any great amount of consideration, although you give it. You are tolerably satisfied with what comes your way, if you do not see any possible way of gaining more, and you do not fret and beat your life out as does the ordinary Pisces person. Whatever else is denied you, you generally win and hold the respect of all your acquaintances, and you deserve it. You have a sort of "happy-go-lucky" way that looks for everything to turn out about right, and this trait gives you considerable satisfaction, whatever may be the effect on your more positive and forceful conjugal companion, who may sometimes show some impatience at the way in which you allow yourself to be put upon. But conscious of the fact that you are doing the best you can, even this does not disturb you much, for you are not so much given to fretting out your life as the ordinary Pisces character.

March 19, 20, 21.

The close proximity of Aries gives you much keenness of perception, and some fire in your composition. Your affectional nature is strong, but you are masterful, dictatorial, sometimes impatient with your children. Still you prefer the obedience that springs from love, rather than that which is enforced, and, you have much affection for your children in addition to a reasonable amount of pride in their ability. You are at times patient with them, and less disturbed by their activity.

You like good living and plenty of it, and although you can come down to close rations, it is from necessity rather than choice. But a moderate amount of prosperity, if not mixed up with too much of the treadmill of life, answers your purpose. But it often happens that some mysterious force chains these later Pisces people down to a condition of toil and labor from which they seldom completely escape,—until perhaps late in life.

Note 1.

These readings are not formulated from any study of individuals. They are the result of close investigation of the characteristics found to belong to certain divisions of each sign. There may be apparent contradictions when brought into comparison with certain lives, but this is only apparent. Down deep in the inner nature they will be found to be correct. For there are many forces that work on each individual life that may turn the direction of its outer manifestation. Circumstances change things. The millionaire may not steal a loaf of bread, or rob an orchard, or plunder a junk shop, for he has no need of this. He may,—often does—plunder a whole community, however. But strip him of his wealth, and bind him down to a condition of grinding poverty, and he will pilfer.

And passing the question of Karmic law, or the results of former incarnations, a man may,—often does—change his life direction, or have it changed for him. Saul of Tarsus started out for Damascus with a certain intent, but he got interfered with on the way. There are no more absolutely honest and law-abiding men in the community than the inmates of our prisons and reformatories, but what keeps them so? Simply an external condition that masters interior desire. And there are walls, and locks and bars, that are not physical.

Now some one has questioned the reading of February 12th, asking if that is the noble Lincoln. Who knows? Who knows aught of the life of our master between his twelfth and thirteenth year? But does any one care to assert that the Lincoln who sat down in the presidential chair in March, 1861, was the Lincoln who entered glory in April, 1865? In a conversation with a friend, speaking of his visit to Gettysburg after the Southern army was driven away, he said, "Standing on that ground I became a changed man—a Christian." Of his early life, certainly his *inner* life, little is known,—probably nothing, for a man's biography is written from his external actions. It is not infrequently the case, that *God* lays his hand on a man's past and sinks it out of sight. And there is many a man who can truly say, *"Non sum qualis eram;"*—I am not *now* what I was.

Note 2.

The somewhat dark and forbidding delineation given under your date must not discourage or dishearten you. Man may become master of himself, and even if his lower traits erect "steps up to heaven." The promises of the Book of Revelation are made "to him that overcometh." And of these promises none stands out more hopefully than that addressed to those whose inner characters are symbolized by Thyatira, "To him that overcometh will I give authority—full dominion over the nations," and "nations" stands for all that is in a man's soul, whether good or evil.

Note 3.

We may not always read one's character truly at the first acquaintance, and may have reason for curtailing the admiration which we hold regarding an individual. But it is well for you to remember,—*unless you wish to set a low estimate on your own judgment,*—that there must have been some good and worthy traits about him or her that attracted you. And think that,—although like the image of Nebuchadnezzar's dream,—the feet and legs were of baser substance, the head was of pure gold, and the breast and arms were of silver.

Note 4.

It is not necessary as a general thing to advise one against critical self-examination, but this nature furnishes an exception. Too much rigid self-immolation might create a morbid condition of mind. Come out more into the light, and love and be loved.

Note 5.

Perhaps you think that Scorpio gets a terrible roasting, but the writer thinks he knows the individual, as he himself is placed in this sign,—October 30th., and fully aware of what possibilities belong to it, and the effort necessary to develop those possibilities; he knows also how the lazy inaction of this nature operates. And so, Brother and Sister Scorpio, console yourself with the knowledge that the castigation falls on the castigator, fully illustrating the saying, "The hand that smites thee is thine own." Therefore, my dear brother or sister, let us pass under the rod together.

Note 6.

Nearly all Sagittarians have a very satisfactory way of giving information or advice, and that without interfering with the freedom of the individual. But some mentors are determined that the person whom they essay to advise *shall* shape his or her course according to the advice, and will often insist on bothering the man at the helm, tipping the compass upside down, overhauling the ballast, thereby destroying their usefulness, and becoming nuisances that the advised must throw overboard to get rid of. Sagittarius people should know their great ability in the way of almost perfect advisers and helpers, and study to cultivate this grand gift, that is so much neglected by them.

Note 7.

The general reader will not care for this last suggestion, as people know little of the general science of Astrology. But I will let it stand, thinking—and hoping—that you will be led to investigate, which, if you are a true Aries individual, you will be tolerably sure to do, for Aries is ravenous for knowledge, and willing to share it with others.

Note 8.

Just here mention should be made of one power possessed by Pisces people, which should have been noticed at the commencement, and that is the power of relieving pain by laying on of the hand. They possess this power in almost as great a degree as Scorpio, with this difference, that while Scorpio's magnetism is positive, reconstructive, masterful, the magnetism of Pisces is soothing, sedative, restful. For this reason a Pisces healer may meet with greater success in cases of intense nervous derangement than Scorpio,—at the outset—for the powerful magnetism of Scorpio is sometimes painful at the first. But the deep seated disease may baffle Pisces in the end, while it yields at last to the intense determination of Scorpio. But the very touch of Pisces brings peace. At least this is the opinion of the writer, founded on experience and observation. Try it, my Pisces friend, for the gift is a diffusive one in your tribe, and see if this theory does not find verification with you. And Cancer people of the middle degrees possess this power.

Diseases of the Various Signs

The Cause.

"We have discovered that disease is the result of misdirected thought, an inverted current turned upon ourselves with force of which we have but little comprehension.

The Remedy.

Lies in realization of the universal life and our personal relation to it. We must change our mental attitude, demagnetize our thought."—"All our prisons are mental. Smith gives us the pass-key to all doors, the control of all environment, deliverance. from all injustice and disease."

Doubtless the reader has noticed that the writer has not mentioned the list of diseases supposed to be peculiar to each sign. The reason is that it is a question whether there is any sufficient basis for this belief. It is easy enough to read up on the subject, and repeat, parrot-like, the words of others. But the writer has a fair amount of Scorpio doubt in his mental make-up, and is in the habit of requiring unimpeachable evidence of the truth of a thing before he labels it and puts it in his cabinet for use. This evidence, so far as he is concerned, may be either material or spiritual; in the latter case it is his own affair. But with the experience of the past thirteen years, during which, for him, medical diagnosis (with its attendant therapeutics), and Astrological science, have been thoroughly welded together, he has seen nothing to convince him that solar influence—so far as it concerns the mental or spiritual make-up—has anything whatever to do with the tendency or liability to particular *physical* ailments. That planetary aspects and influences are a potent factor in causing, developing and augmenting disease, he believes as firmly and completely as he believes in his own existence. And even the position of the sun—*as a centre of planetary activity*—is a part of the problem, and influences the outer, manifest mental and physical life according to its place in one's horoscope as much as do its attendant planets. However, the sun, by virtue of a mysterious law of correspondence, is far more than this, but the operation of this law, which governs the universe from THE CREATOR down to the veriest minutiæ of created matter, is too deep and vast a subject to consider now and here.

The professional experience of the writer runs counter to the general teaching of Astrological writers. He has met with as many cases of lung, heart and bowel disorders in Aries and Pisces people as with Cancer, Leo, and Virgo, which are considered as peculiarly liable to these disorders, and as many cases of brain distemper and diseases of the lower limbs in Leo, Virgo and Cancer people as with Aries and Pisces. And that consummate nuisance, Rheumatism, is no respector of persons, or parts, but explodes on neck, chest, arms, back, legs and feet, without evincing any particular choice of any one.

Furthermore, there is no medical data on which to found this assumption. A very small percentage of medical practitioners know anything whatever of Astrology, and those who do are very reticent regarding it. In fact, if one wants to find the most perfect reproduction of the modern Nicodemus, let him run up against a doctor who believes in planetary influence in matters of disease, and who calls Astrological science to his aid in his diagnosis. You will be very certain to find that individual pursuing his investigations and holding his consultation by candle light, and he is apt to blow out the candle if any one knocks at the door. It's all right, brother practitioner; there are some revelations that the world is not yet ready for. Your humble servant has learned that fact through some rebuffs and set-backs, and gives his advice in this direction—free.

And so, in the absence of medical data, the writer is compelled to be an agnostic on this point. He does not deny, but only questions. The opinions of Astrological writers are worth *what they are worth,* but it is a suggestive fact to him that, so far as his acquaintance with these writers extends, only one writer on Astrology—the late Dr. L. D. Broughton, New York—was or is a practicing physician, and therefore the conceptions and teachings of these—many of them able and intelligent men—do not rest on any basis of experience. That grand old Mystic, Paracelsus, and the quaint Nicholas Culpeper, while uncompromising and unflinching believers in planetary influence on disease and remedy, have nothing to say about sign diseases.

And it is this aspect of the subject that has led the writers to omit all reference to any connection between zodiacal signs and disease, being impressed with the conviction that there is as yet more in the realm of *fact* than the average man is ready to admit, without entering into the domain of uncertain *speculation*. With which agnostic confession he feels like dismissing the question, while ready for further light, from without or within.

And one more fallacy may as well be noticed here, and that is, the supposition that there are lucky or unlucky days. These calculations belong entirely to horary astrology, and are judged according to the aspects of the planets. For instance, suppose you were born in Sagittarius or Pisces. Your ruling planet in that case is Jupiter. Now, any day on which Jupiter is in good aspect with the sun and not afflicted by either Saturn or Mars, and in Sagittarius, Pisces or Cancer, would be a good day to start any business project. But if Jupiter is in Capricorn or Virgo and in evil aspect to Saturn or Mars, especially the latter planet, it would be a most unfortunate day for your project. But these aspects do not occur the *same day* in *any* year, and what might be a fortunate day this year would be a most unfortunate one next year. These calculations can be made only with the aid of an ephemeris and working of "directions." For this reason all allusion to "lucky days" is omitted in this book, and the reader is advised not to pay the least attention to any such pretense. The grand science of Astrology has suffered full enough, according to the writer's opinion, without any such exploiting by him. That these prognostications can be easily worked out by any honest, conscientious astrologer is a fact, as any one can easily find out if he wishes. But it is a use of Astrology which the writer has very little sympathy with, and does not practice. There is a line between Astrology and Necromancy, which he considers it well to keep away from.

And in regard to the claim that persons born in the various signs have the same physical characteristics, the writer holds the same opinion. There is no basis for this claim that he has ever discovered. Within a hundred yards of his office are four children of different families, ages from nine to thirteen years. They were all born between the fifth and ninth of August. One is dark and swarthy, with coarse, curly hair and black eyes, slim figure; one dark and clear with brown straight hair and brown eyes, and stout build; one with straight, light sandy hair, very light complexion, red cheeks, very light gray eyes, very slim figure; and one stout, indifferent complexion, light brown hair, and very light hazel eyes, verging on blue. Which of these physiques indicates Leo? But the horoscopes of these four children, which the writer worked out with the utmost care, clearly indicate that the external appearance is stamped by the sign that is rising at the time of birth, and not the sign the sun is in. Although if this sign happens to be rising at birth, its influence will be stamped unmistakably on the face and form.

Friendships and Conjugal Mates

ARIES:—MARCH 22 TO APRIL 20.

Your best conjugal mates are Leo and Sagittarius people. You may do well in your own sign,—certainly you will find pleasant companions there.

TAURUS:—APRIL 21 TO MAY 21.

Taurus people find their most congenial conjugal partners in Virgo and Capricorn, and not unfrequently in Libra.

GEMINI:—MAY 22 TO JUNE 22.

You will find true, helpful, devoted friends in Virgo and Aries, but your conjugal mate, if you find one, will be best if in Libra, Aquarius, or your own sign.

CANCER:—JUNE 23 TO JULY 22.

The Cancer man can find a congenial mate in Pisces, Virgo, or Libra, sometimes, *but not often,* a perfect mate in Scorpio. But if you you are a Cancer *woman* be sure of your mutual adaptedness before you fix your state, and thus save yourself future unhappiness,—possibly disaster. Pisces or Cancer will furnish your best mate. One writer asserts that a single life is to be preferred for Cancer women. The author, however, does not believe in this theory for any created being, man, woman or angel.

LEO:—JULY 23 TO AUGUST 23.

The Leo woman finds her best conjugal mate in Aries,—the Leo man finds his in Aries or Sagittarius.

VIRGO:—AUGUST 24 TO SEPTEMBER 23.

You will find congenial friends and associates in Libra and Sagittarius, although the latter will not take your spanking patiently at the time, but he will come back for your sympathy again when he needs it, and take the risk of another castigation. Your best marital companion will be found in your own sign, Virgo. although you may find one in Libra or Sagittarius.

LIBRA:—SEPTEMBER 24 TO OCTOBER 23.

You can find congenial companions and associates in almost any sign, but your best conjugal partners are found in your own sign, and in Aquarius and Virgo. Those in the first part of the sign had better steer clear of Scorpio and Taurus, for while the men of these signs have a strength and will power that attracts the women of nearly every cusp, they are apt to prove impatient, and much discontent and unhappiness ensue. The woman of the middle and latter degrees of Libra, however, have a force and strength that blend well with Scorpio, and often masters and reforms it, and their common love for the mysterious and occult often links them together in firm and affectionate bonds.

SCORPIO:—OCTOBER 24 TO NOVEMBER 22.

As to associates, Virgo people will prove true friends, as they will mercilessly puncture your bubbles of pretense, but in a kindly way, and "faithful are the wounds of a friend." As connubial partners, your most congenial ones will be found in Cancer, for these people have the loving, tender nature that alone can *lead* Scorpio, for it cannot be *driven* except to a perdition from which it may take it a long time to emerge. Warm attachments may indeed exist between Scorpio and Pisces, but they need an occasional vacation. Scorpio wearies of the fretting, worrying, *weeping* manifestations of Pisces, which its own harshness and unfeeling thoughtlessness tend often to stimulate and augment. Your conjugal partner par excellence—if you are a Scorpio man—will be found in Cancer. Perhaps a Virgo woman would exactly fit the better developed Scorpio man. The Scorpio woman will find a helpful companion in Virgo, or Libra, or even in her own sign.

SAGATTARIUS:—NOVEMBER 23 TO DECEMBER 22.

You find congenial associates in Aries, Leo, and Libra, sometimes in Scorpio. Your most fitting marital companion comes from Leo or Aquarius, sometimes Libra.

CAPRICORN:—DECEMBER 23 TO JANUARY 20.

Your general faculty of adapting yourself to every condition, friend Capricorn, will insure you congenial friends among people of every sign, but for the more interior friendships and a conjugal companion look to Virgo, Taurus or Libra.

AQUARIUS:—JANUARY 21 TO FEBRUARY 19.

Congenial companions will be found in Aries and Sagittarius, but your conjugal partner is found in Aquarius.

Pisces:—February 20 to March 21.

Capricorn and Virgo furnish you many congenial companions. As a marital companion, if you are a Pisces woman, a Cancer man would suit you best. If a Pisces man, the positive strength of Virgo or Capricorn would be nearer your need, but the Cancer woman, unless strengthened by polarization and planetary influences, would be too weak for you, and a Scorpio woman would nag and worry your life out of you.

A Final Word to the Reader

Perhaps, my dear reader, you may consider that I have taken a wanton liberty in addressing you, in the foregoing delineations, as a personality. But we are most of us so constituted that ordinary generalities do not strike so deeply as a direct *"Thou art the man."* A sin or wrong seems most heinous when portrayed in its naked deformity, and considered as the act of another. But the way to make a man think, and think to the purpose, is to set him face to face with his own soul.

We are, most of us, fully conscious of our best traits, and need not have them indicated. But those interior forces and tendencies that hinder one's soul in its development,—and will continue to be a drag or obstacle to his progress, unless he learns how, under a higher guidance, to make them serve his nobler aspirations and purpose—these, it seems to the writer, are the things to be emphasized.

And then much depends upon how one looks at these things of the inner life, which the dogmatic theology stigmatizes as "evils," for nothing is evil until one makes it so. The steam in the boiler is a dangerous element. You need the steam gauge to indicate the pressure, and the safety valve to relieve undue energy and free the surplus. But you cannot drive your engine without it. What you need is some knowledge of the laws of action of steam, and how to apply and control its energies. With this knowledge, and the testing of experience in regard to the strength of the boiler, the man is, to all intents and purposes, practically safe.

There is nothing more dangerous and destructive than misunderstood and misapplied power. THE CREATOR has endowed every man and woman with a certain amount of power—stored him or her with some form of energy. To know one's own self, to understand how to direct, control, apply this energy, is well worth one's study. We may indeed learn by our failures, but they weaken us.

This work deals entirely with the solar influences on the nature, the inner life that controls the manifestations of the outer life. In this regard we are, to a certain extent, creatures of fate—vessels made according to the design—aye, the intention of the potter. It is for each individual to find his highest use, and fit himself for it. Planetary influences play upon us in varied, possibly antagonistic ways, but these influences may be studied and frustrated. This is the meaning of the proverb, "The wise man *rules* his stars; the fool *obeys* them." But this subtle life principle which flows into the inner life, and remains a latent energy until the movement of *conscious* life calls it into activity, is a pervading, ever present, ever active reality that cannot be repressed.

And therefore in this little book the author chooses to take your hand, and look into your eye, and talk to you as an individual personality. The result of his labor, the fruit of his study and investigation, all that experience has taught him, he tenders to you personally, so far as it serves your own personal uses and needs, as he holds your hand in friendly grasp and bids you an affectionate ADIEU AND GODSPEED.

"Swift years, but teach me how to bear,
  To feel, to act, with strength and skill,
To reason wisely, nobly dare,
  Then speed your courses as you will."

"When life's meridian toils are done,
  How calm, how rich, the twilight glow!
The morning twilight of a sun
  That shines not on these things below."

"Press onward through each varying hour;
  Let no weak fears thy course delay;
Immortal being, feel thy power;
  Pursue thy bright and endless way."

Lucky or Fortunate Days

It is the desire of the publishers that in this, and subsequent editions of this book, some directions for deciding on fortunate days be given, and therefore this chapter is added. It is possible to give, however, only a brief treatment of this subject, as it would increase the size of the book too much were we to go deeply into this matter.

Every sign is governed by some planet, as follows:—

ARIES and SCORPIO by MARS.
TAURUS and LIBRA by VENUS.
GEMINI and VIRGO by MERCURY.
CANCER by the MOON.
LEO by the SUN.
SAGATTARIUS and PISCES by JUPITER.
CAPRICORN by SATURN.
AQUARIUS by URANUS.

There are also certain signs in which planets are strong, or weak;—noting that every planet is strongest in the signs which it governs. The exaltation, detriment, or fall of each is as follows:

The SUN is strong in *Aries;* weak in *Libra* and *Aquarius.*

The MOON is strong in *Taurus;* weak in *Scorpio* and *Capricorn.*

MERCURY is strong in *Virgo;* weak in *Sagittarius* and *Pisces.*

VENUS is strong in *Pisces;* weak in *Aries, Virgo* and *Scorpio.*

MARS is strong in *Capricorn;* weak in *Taurus, Cancer* and *Libra.*

JUPITER is strong in *Cancer;* weak in *Gemini, Virgo* and *Capricorn.*

SATURN is strong in *Libra;* weak in *Aries* and *Cancer.*

URANUS is strong in *Scorpio;* weak in *Taurus* and *Leo.*

When one's ruling planet,—the planet ruling his sign,—is in a sign where it is strong, matters will run fairly smoothly, unless said planet is afflicted, which will be explained later on. There are some aspects which are favorable, and others unfavorable. The favorable aspects are the *Trine* (△), *Sextile* (✱), *Semi-sextile* (⚺), and sometimes the *Conjunction* (☌). The unfavorable aspects are the *Square* (□), *Semi-square* (∠), *Opposition* (☍) and sometimes the *Conjunction* (☌). The conjunction of *Saturn* with any planet except *Jupiter* is unfavorable. All conjunctions of *Mars* are unfavorable. Suppose you were born May 1st. The *Sun* is in *Taurus,* and you belong to that sign, which is governed by *Venus.* Now, when *Venus* is in *Taurus, Libra,* or *Pisces,* especially if any planet is in *Trine, Sextile, Semi-sextile* to it, or the *Moon* in conjunction with it, you will find matters generally satisfactory. But if any planet is *Square, Semi-Square,* or in *Opposition* to *Venus,* you will not find things so satisfactory. If *Venus* is in *Aries, Virgo,* or *Scorpio,* you can generally look for some vexations, and if any planet, *Saturn* or *Mars* especially, come to a *Square, Opposition,* or *Conjunction* with her during her debilitation in these signs, look for trouble, and disarrangements of love affairs. If *Jupiter* is your ruler, guard your finances. If *Mars* is your ruler, look out for accidents. If *Mercury* rules your sign, it indicates quarrels. If the *Moon* is your ruler, guard your health. If the *Sun* rules your sign, fever or accident is indicated. If *Saturn,* you may make some bad mistakes in judgment.

If either *Venus* or *Jupiter* enter your sign, it is a help in a general way. *Saturn* or *Mars,* unless you are ruled by one of these planets, coming into your sign, means mischief. As the *Moon* passes through the Zodiac every twenty-eight days, the aspects of this planet alternate more frequently than the others.

Some almanacs give the planetary aspects in the calendar. "The Old Farmer's Almanac" used to give them very completely, but "Raphaels' Ephemeris," published annually in London, gives them with great accuracy. With the aid of this publication,—especially if the Astrological Almanac (price 35 cents), is combined with it,—you can easily work out these little details.

This, of course, is only an outline, and a very incomplete one at that, for it requires much knowledge of Astrology to work out horary questions,—that is, matters of daily life and interest. The time has been when the wisest men called this science to their aid; doubtless it will come again. Raphaels' Ephemerides for the last two years contain a complete aspectarian,—or list of planetary aspects for every day of the year. It is a valuable addition. No other ephemeris that the writer knows of, has this feature.

Raphaels' Almanac for 1904 has one page devoted to some severe strictures on the issuing of so-called "Test Horoscopes." The author has seen several of these non-descripts and fully agrees with Raphael in his criticism of them. They seem put out as baits for further business. Those that I have seen are simply ready-made garments, got up to fit everybody, and which fit nobody. They are readings culled from various works,—largely condensations from Butler's Solar Biology, and based on the general effects of the Sun in certain signs. A note at the end of each suggests that planetary influences may change or almost nullify the reading of the "test horoscope," and advising the recipient to have a full horoscope. Any one who never heard of astrology can issue these papers with the aid of Eleanor Kirk's "Influence of the Zodiac." They really tell nothing of value. All people born in certain signs are not alike, any more than all inhabitants of New York City are alike. There may be certain similar characteristics, but there is more to astrological science than this.

Birth Dates of Celebrated Men and Women

ARIES:—MARCH 22 TO APRIL 20.
Who on this world of ours their eyes
In Aries open, shall be wise,
In days of peril firm and brave,
And wear an Amethyst to their graves.

	Date.	Year.
Sir Anthony Vandyke (Flemish Painter)	22	1599
Dr. James M. Peebles (Pioneer Spiritualist)	23	1822
Richard A. Proctor (Astronomer)	23	1837
George Francis Train (Author and Financier)	24	1829
Michael Davitt (Irish Agitator)	25	1846
David Brainerd Lyman (Preacher)	27	1840
La Place (Astronomer)	28	1749
John Tyler (President U. S.)	29	1790
Frank Leslie (Publisher)	29	1821
Rene Descartes (Philosopher)	31	1596
John La Farge (Artist)	31	1835
Joseph Haydn (Composer)	31	1732
Prince Bismarck (German General)	1	1815
Thomas Jefferson (President U. S.)	2	1743
Emile Zola (French Writer and Patriot)	2	1840
Hans Christian Andersen (Author)	2	1805
John Burroughs (Naturalist and Author)	3	1837
Edward Everett Hale (Clergyman and Author)	3	1822
Washington Irving (Author)	3	1783
Thaddeus Stevens (Statesman)	4	1792
Joseph Medill (Journalist)	6	1823
Bishop Nicholas Matz (R. C. Bishop)	6	1850
Raphael (Painter)	6	1483
William Wordsworth (Poet)	7	1770
William Ellery Channing (Liberal Preacher)	7	1780

David Rittenhouse (Astronomer)	8	1732
King Leopold II (Belgian King)	9	1835
General Booth (Salvationist)	10	1829
Henry Clay (Statesman and Orator)	12	1777
James Harper (Founder of Publishing House)	13	1795
Cardinal Vaughan (of London)	15	1832
John Lothrop Motley (Historian and Diplomat)	15	1821
George M. N. Yost (Inventor of Typewriter)	15	1831
Charles J. Folger (Judge and Politician)	16	1818
J. Pierpont Morgan (Financier)	17	1837
Dr. Chas. H. Parkhurst (Reformer)	17	1842
Chas. M. Schwab (Capitalist and Promoter)	18	1862
Wayne MacVeagh (Lawyer and Politician)	19	1833
John Lloyd (Chemist and Author)	19	1849

TAURUS:—APRIL 21 TO MAY 21.

Those who in Taurus date their years,
Moss Agate should wear, lest bitter tears
For vain repentance flow. This stone
Emblem of innocence is known.

	Date.	Year.
Charlotte Bronte (Author)	21	1816
Ada Rehan (Actress)	22	1859
Carter H. Harrison (Politician)	23	1860
Sen. Chauncey M. Depew (R. R. Pres. and Sen.)	23	1834
William Shakespeare (Dramatist and Poet)	23	1564
James Buchanan (Pres. U. S.)	23	1791
William Deering (Manufacturer)	25	1826
Oliver Cromwell (Prime Minister of England)	25	1599
Hon. Benj. F. Tracy (Politician)	26	1830
Baroness Burdett-Coutts (Eccentric Eng. Lady)	26	1814
Kossuth	27	1802
Herbert Spencer (Scientific Philosopher)	27	1820
Gen. U. S. Grant (Pres. U. S.)	27	1822
Palmer Cox (Brownie Man)	28	1840
James Monroe (Pres. U. S.)	28	1758
Dr. Hiram S. Thomas (Philanthropist & Preacher)	29	1832
Sir John Lubbock (Scientist)	30	1834
Duke of Wellington (Hero at Waterloo)	1	1769
Joseph Addison (Poet and Author)	1	1672
Marie Corelli (One of World's Greatest Writers)	1	——

Albion W. Tourgee (Author-Journalist)........	2	1838
Queen Natalie	2	1859
Charles Samuel Deneen (Politician)............	4	1863
William H. Prescott (Author)..................	4	1796
Elmer Gates (Inventor and Scientist)..........	5	1859
Hubert Howe Bancroft (Historian)............	5	1832
John McCutcheon (Illustrator)...............	6	1870
Lieutenant R. E. Peary (Arctic Explorer)........	6	1856
Dante (Author)	8	1265
Frank G. Carpenter (Traveler and Correspondent).	8	1855
John Brown (Abolitionist)....................	9	1800
Walter de Voe (Philosopher and Teacher).......	11	1874
Elizabeth Towne (Thinker-Publisher of Nautilus).	11	——
Timothy Dwight (Pres. of Yale)..............	14	1752
Levi P. Morton (Financier and Statesman)......	16	1824
Philip D. Armour (Merchant and Philanthropist).	16	1832
John W. Gates (Capitalist)..................	18	1855
Nicholas II (Czar of Russia).................	18	1868
Madame Nelle Melba (Prima Donna)...........	19	1865

GEMINI:—MAY 22 TO JUNE 22.
Who first beholds the light of day
In Spring's sweet sign of Gemini,
And will wear a Beryl all her life,
Shall be a loved and happy wife.

	Date.	Year.
Conan Doyle (Author)........................	22	1859
Richard Wagner (Musical Composer)..........	22	1813
Queen Victoria (English Queen)...............	24	1819
Stephen Girard (Merchant and Philanthropist)..	24	1750
John Alexander Dowie (Elijah II).............	25	1837
Ralph Waldo Emerson (Poet and Philosopher)...	25	1803
Edward Livingston (Jurist and Statesman)......	26	1764
Nathaniel Green (Hero of Revolution).........	27	1742
Julia Ward Howe (Author Battle Hymn of Rep.).	27	1819
Jay Gould (Railway Builder and Capitalist)......	27	1836
Sir Thomas Moore (Irish Poet)................	28	1779
Patrick Henry (Statesman and Orator).........	29	1736
Walt Whitman (Poet and Philosopher).........	31	1819
William Rockefeller (Pres. Standard Oil Co.)....	31	1841
Cynthia M. W. Alden (Founder of Sunshine Club)	31	1862

Brigham Young (Mormon)	1	1801
William E. Curtis (News Correspondent)	1	1855
Pope Pius X	2	1835
Bishop J. L. Spalding (Liberal R. C. Bishop)	2	1840
Jefferson Davis (Pres. of Confederacy)	3	1808
Walter L. Deane (Marine Painter)	4	1854
George T. Angell (Founder Humane Society)	5	1823
Nathan Hale (Revolutionary Patriot)	6	1755
Susan E. Blow (Kindergartner)	7	1843
Robert Schumann	8	1810
David Porter (2nd. Admiral U. S. Navy)	8	1813
John Howard Payne (Author of "Home Sweet Home.")	9	1791
Sir Edwin Arnold (Author-Poet)	10	1832
Harriet Beecher Stowe ("Uncle Tom's Cabin")	14	1811
Paul Rembrandt (Dutch Painter)	15	1606
John Wesley (Founder of Methodism)	17	1703
Baron Von Humboldt (Astronomer)	21	1767

CANCER:—June 23 to July 22.
Who comes with summer to this earth,
And owes to Cancer her day of birth,
With ring of Emerald on her hand
Can health, wealth and peace command.

	Date	Year
Stuyvesant Fish (Financier)	24	1851
Charles T. Yerkes (Organizer and Financier)	25	1837
Lord Kelvin (Astronomer)	26	1824
Jean Jacques Rousseau (French Writer)	28	1712
Rubens (Painter)	29	1577
Sir Robert Ball (Astronomer)	1	1840
Richard Henry Stoddard (Poet)	2	1825
Robert Ridgway (Naturalist)	2	1850
Nathaniel Hawthorne (Author)	4	1804
John Gunzenhauser (Pioneer Real Estate Chicago)	5	1833
William T. Stead (Ed. Eng. Review of Reviews)	5	1849
Admiral Farragut (1st. Admiral U. S. Navy)	5	1801
Prof. Daniel Coit Gilman (Pres. Carnegie Inst.)	6	1831
Sen. William Ernest Mason (Philanthropist)	7	1850
John D. Rockefeller (Founder of Univ. of Chicago)	8	1839
Fitz-Greene Halleck (Poet)	8	1790

Florence Marryat (Author)	9	1837
John Calvin (Reformer)	10	1509
John Quincy Adams (Pres. U. S.)	11	1767
John Wanamaker (Merchant)	11	1837
Dr. Cyrenius Wakefield (Found. Wakefield Co.) .	12	1815
Sen. Thomas Collier Platt (Pres. Am. Exp. Co.) ..	15	1833
Mary Baker G. Eddy (Found. Christian Science) .	16	1821
Sir Joshua Reynolds (Portrait Painter)	16	1722
Dr. Paul Carus (Edit. Monist & Open Court Mag.)	18	1852

Leo:—July 23 to August 23.
The glowing Ruby should adorn
Those in sultry Leo born;
Thus will they be exempt and free
From Love's doubts and anxiety.

	Date	Year
Cardinal James Gibbons (2nd Cardinal in U. S.) ..	23	1834
Dr. Albert Shaw (Editor)	23	1857
Pres. William R. Harper (Pres. Univ. of Chicago).	26	1856
George Barr McCutcheon (Journalist-Cartoonist) .	26	1861
Mary Anderson (Navarro—formerly Actress)	28	1859
Horatio W. Seymour (Ed. Chicago Chronicle)	29	1854
Max Nordau (Author)	29	1849
John V. Farwell (Merchant & Philanthropist)	29	1825
Robert J. Burdett (Journalist & Humorist)	30	1844
Paul Du Chaillu (Explorer and Author)	31	1835
Hon. Robt. Todd Lincoln (Statesman)	1	1843
Francis Marion Crawford (Author)	2	1854
Eugene Murray Aaron (Scientist)	4	
Russell Sage (Financier & Promoter)	4	1816
Percy Bysshe Shelley (Poet, Philosopher)	4	1792
Marquis of Lorne (Gov. Gen. of Canada)	6	1845
Daniel O'Connell (Irish Patriot)	6	1775
Chas. A. Dana (Ed. New York Sun)	8	1819
Major Gen. Nelson A. Miles (U. S. Army)	8	1839
John Dryden (Poet)	9	1631
Joseph Pulitzer (Founder New York World)	10	1847
Robt. G. Ingersoll (Lawyer, Orator)	11	1833
Robert Southey (Poet)	12	1774
Mrs. Lucy Stone (Reformer)	13	1818

Felix Adler (Educator, Ethical Culture Society)..13 1851
Henry Clews (Financier and Banker)..........14 1840
Sir Walter Scott (Author, Poet of Scotland)....15 1771
Napoleon Bonaparte (Emperor of France)......15 1808
Kwang-Hsu (Emperor of China) 15 1871
Archbishop M. A. Corrigan (Organizer)........17 1839
Cardinal Rampolla (Rome) 17 1843
Charles Francis Adams (Statesman)............18 1807
Marshall Field (Merchant) 18 1835
James Lenox (Founder of Lenox Liby).........19 1800
Elizabeth Stuart 19 1596
Benj. Harrison (Pres. U. S.) 20 1833
Frank A. Munsey (Pub. of Magazine, Author)...21 1854
Oliver H. Perry (Hero of Battle of Lake Erie)...21 1785
Prof. Wm. Pepper (Philosopher & Physician)....21 1843
John R. Walsh (Banker, Pub. Philanthropist)...22 1837
John B. Gough (Temperance Lecturer).........22 1817
Amelie Reeves Chanler (Author)..............23 1863

VIRGO:—August 24 to September 23.
Wear a Jasper, or for thee
No conjugal felicity;
The Virgo born without this stone,
'Tis said, must live unloved, alone.

Date Year

Theodore Parker (Preacher, Writer, Reformer)..24 1810
Francis Bret Harte (Author, Poet)............25 1839
Prince Albert (Consort of Queen Victoria)......26 1819
M. A. DeWolfe Howe (Staff of Youths Companion 28 1864
Johann Wolfgang Goethe (Composer, Poet).....28 1749
Archbishop Patrick Feehan (Roman Catholic)....29 1829
Charles Howard Shinn (Editor, Writer)........20 1852
Oliver Wendell Holmes (Physician, Author)....29 1809
Hon. David B. Hill (Politician, Gov. of N. Y.)..29 1843
Hazen S. Pingree (Gov. Michigan)............30 1840
Geo. F. Root (Composer "Battle Cry of Freedom") 30 1820
Queen Wilhelmina (Netherlands) 31 1880
James Gordon Bennett (Founder of N. Y. Herald) 1 1795
Peter Cartwright (Orig. of M. E. Camp-meetings) 1 1785

Eugene Field (Journalist-Poet)	2	1850
Murat Halstead (Journalist-Author)	2	1829
Luther Laflin Mills (Lawyer-Lecturer)	3	1848
John G. Carlisle (Sec'y of Treas. under Cleveland)	5	1835
La Fayette (Revolutionary Friend of America)	6	1757
Victorien Sardou (Writer of Plays)	7	1831
Emilio Castelar (Astronomer, Writer)	8	1832
Count Leon Tolstoi (Philosopher-Writer)	9	1828
Archbishop John Ireland (Orator)	11	1838
Right Rev. John Joseph Keane (Roman Catholic)	12	1839
Henry Cornelius Agrippa (Philosopher-Mystic)	14	1486
Hon. Richard Olney (Sec'y State under Cleveland)	15	1835
Wm. H. Taft (Gov. Phillippines)	15	1857
Gen. Porfirio Diaz (Pres. Mexico)	15	1830
James Hill (Pres. Northern Pacific R. R.)	16	1828
James Bowdoin (Founder of Bowdoin College)	22	1752
Wm. DeWitt Hyde (Pres. Bowdoin College)	23	1858
Grace Greenwood	23	1823

LIBRA:—September 24 to October 23.

A maiden born when Autumn's leaves
Are rustling in lovely Libra's breeze,
Diamonds on her brow should bind;
'Twill cure diseases of the mind.

	Date	Year
John Marshall (Chief Justice U. S.)	24	1755
Marcus A. Hanna (Merchant, Senator-Philan.)	24	1837
Cardon (Astrologer, Alchemist)	24	1501
Zackary Taylor (Pres. U. S.)	24	1784
Felicia Dorothea Hemans (Poet-Writer)	25	1793
Thomas Nast (Cartoonist)	27	1840
Frances E. Willard (Reformer. President W. C. T. U.)	28	1839
Lord Nelson (British Admiral)	29	1758
Senator Matthew S. Quay (U. S. Senator)	30	1833
Samuel S. Cox (Statesman)	30	1824
Annie Besant (Theosophist, Writer, Lecturer)	1	1847
Lilian Whiting (Author-Journalist)	3	1857
Guizot (French Historian)	4	1787
Rutherford B. Hayes (Pres. U. S.)	4	1822

Chester A. Arthur (Pres. U. S.)	5	1830
Eleanor Kirk Ames (Eleanor Kirk's Idea)	7	1830
Edmund Clarence Stedman (Poet and Critic)	8	1833
Hon. Col. John Hay (Author and Statesman)	8	1838
Cervantes (Author of "Don Quixote")	9	1547
Rowland G. Hazard (Mfr. and Author)	9	1801
Michael Von Munkacsy (Painter)	10	1846
Fridtjof Nansen (Polar Explorer)	10	1861
Ex-Pres. Paul Kruger (South African Republic)	10	1825
Theodore Thomas (Mus. Dir. and Composer)	11	1835
Hugh Miller (Naturalist)	12	1802
Helena Modjeska (Polish Actress)	12	1844
William Penn (Founder of Pa.)	14	1644
Albert L. Rawson (Founder of Theoso. Society, U. S.)	15	1828
James Edward Quigley (R. C. Bishop)	15	1854
Freeman B. Dowd (Author-Sage)	15	1828
Samuel Bowles (Springfield Republican)	15	1851
Rev. Sam P. Jones (Evangelist)	16	1847
Hon. Thomas Brackett Reed (Congressman-Author)	18	1839
Daniel Edgar Sickles (Soldier-Politician)	20	1825
Oliver Ditson (Music Publisher)	20	1811
Alphonse de Lamartine (Poet-Historian)	21	1790
Sarah Bernhardt (French Actress)	22	1844
Edward Wallace Conable ("Pathfinder")	23	——

Scorpio—October 24 to November 22.

Scorpio's child is born for woe,
And Life's vicissitudes must know;
But lay a Topaz on her breast,
And hope will lull the woes to rest.

	Date	Year
Macaulay (English Historian)	25	1800
Edmund Halley (Discoverer Halley's Comet)	26	1656
A. T. Stewart (Merchant)	27	1802
Theodore Roosevelt (Pres. U. S.)	27	1858
Gambetta (Italian Patriot)	30	1838
Dr. J. R. Phelps (Author of this Book)	30	——
Whitelaw Reid (Diplomat. Owner of N. Y. Tribune)	30	1837

Name	Day	Year
Dr. Nicholas Senn (Physician and Surgeon)	31	1844
Dr. Morgan Dix (Preacher)	1	1827
James Knox Polk (Pres. U. S.)	2	1795
Mutsu Hito (Mikado, Japan)	3	1852
Wm. Cullen Bryant (Poet and Editor)	3	1794
John J. Mitchell (Banker and Philanthropist)	3	1853
Benj. F. Butler (Lawyer, Soldier, Politician)	5	1818
Ella Wheeler Wilcox (Poet)	5	1853
Alzamon Ira Lucas (Lecturer)	5	——
Ignace Jan Paderewski (Musician)	6	1860
Dr. Edwin Hartley Pratt (Physician)	6	1849
Perier-Casimir (French Statesman)	8	1847
Gen. O. O. Howard (Major-General)	8	1830
Dr. Alice B. Stockham (Author "Lovers' World")	8	1833
Edward VII. (King of Great Britain and Ireland)	9	1841
Martin Luther (Founder of Lutheranism)	10	1483
Joaquin Miller (Poet of Sierras)	10	1841
Henry Van Dyke (Clergyman and Author)	10	1852
Edward Everett (Harvard President)	11	1794
Elizabeth Cady Stanton (Womans' Rights Advocate)	12	1816
Richard Baxter (English Divine)	12	1615
Robert Louis Stevenson (Author and Correspondent)	13	1850
Duke of Marlborough (Married Amer. Heiress)	13	1871
Albert (Prince of Monaco)	13	1848
Sir William Herschel (Astronomer)	15	1738
William Pitt (English Statesman)	15	1708
John Bright (English Statesman)	16	1811
Emma Thursby (Opera Singer)	17	1857
Gen. Fitzhugh Lee (Soldier and Gov.)	19	1835
James A. Garfield (Pres. U. S.)	19	1831
Voltaire (Writer)	21	1694
Hetty Green (A Rich Woman of World)	21	1835
James H. Eckles (Comptroller under Cleveland)	22	1858
Josiah Dwight Whitney	22	1819
Justin McCarthy (Writer)	22	1830

SAGITTARIUS—November 23 to December 22.

Who first come to this world below
With Sagittarius' fog and snow,
Should prize the Carbuncle, fiery hue,
Emblem of friends and lovers true.

	Date	Year
Franklin Pierce (Pres. U. S.)	23	1804
Frances Hodgson Burnett (Author)	24	1849
Benedict de Spinoza (Philosopher)	24	1632
Andrew Carnegie (Philanthropist)	25	1837
George Cary Eggleston (Author and Editor)	26	1839
William Cowper (Author)	26	1731
Jonathan Swift (Humorist)	30	1667
Samuel L. Clemens (Humorist-Author)	30	1835
Queen Alexandria (England)	1	1844
William H. Holmes (Geologist and Ethnologist	1	1846
Gen. Geo. B. McClellan (War of '61 to '65)	3	1826
Thomas Carlyle (Author and Essayist)	4	1795
Martin Van Buren (Pres. U. S.)	5	1782
Max Mueller (German Scientist)	6	1823
Edwin Southern (Actor)	6	1859
Joel Chandler Harris (Author of "Uncle Remus")	8	1848
Bjornstjerne Bjornson (Author)	8	1832
John Milton (Poet)	9	1608
Edward Eggleston (Clergyman and Literary Ed.)	10	1837
George Goldthwaite (Senator and Jurist)	10	1810
Henry Morton (Scientist)	11	1836
William Lloyd Garrison (Revolutionist)	12	1805
John Jay (Statesman and Jurist)	12	1745
Heinrich Heine (Poet)	13	1799
Phillips Brooks (Preacher)	13	1835
Orson Smith (Banker and Philanthropist)	14	1841
Tycho Brake (Danish Astronomer)	14	1546
Bishop John B. McQuaid (Seaton Hall College)	15	1823
Ludwig Van Beethoven (Composer)	17	1770
John Greenleaf Whittier (Quaker Poet)	17	1807
Th. Ribot (French Scientist)	18	1839
Lyman Abbot (Theologian and Author)	18	1805
Mary A. Livermore (Reformer)	19	1821
Disraeli (Author-Minister of England)	21	1835
Thomas Fitzgerald (Journalist)	22	1816

CAPRICORN—December 23 to January 20.

If cold Capricorn gave you birth,
The sign of snow and ice and mirth,
Place on your hand an Onyx ring,
And success will bless you in everything.

	Date	Year
Samuel Smiles (Author of Self-Help)	23	1812
Matthew Arnold	24	1822
Sir Isaac Newton (Astronomer)	25	1642
Admiral George Dewey (3d Admiral U. S. Navy)	26	1838
Johann Kepler (Astronomer)	27	1751
William E. Gladstone (English Statesman)	29	1809
Andrew Johnson (Pres. U. S.)	29	1808
John P. Altgeld (Politician and Governor)	30	1847
Rudyard Kipling (Author-Writer)	30	1865
President Emile Loubet (Pres. France)	31	1838
Gen. Anthony Wayne (Rev. General)	1	1745
Charles Sumner (Statesman and Orator)	6	1811
Albert Bierstadt (Artist)	7	1830
Gen. James Longstreet (Confederate Gen.)	8	1821
Marshall Ney (French General)	10	1769
Wm. Sear (Capitalist—Boy at 75)	11	1828
Alexander Hamilton (Statesman-Patriot)	11	1757
John Hancock (First Signer of Declaration of Independence)	12	1737
Salmon P. Chase (Chief Justice U. S.)	13	1808
Marquis of Lansdowne (Premier of Canada)	14	1845
Moliere (Actor)	15	1622
August Weismann (Writer-Philosopher)	17	1834
Benj. Franklin (Philosopher-Philanthropist)	17	1706
Daniel Webster (Author of Dictionary)	18	1782
Olga Nethersole (Actress)	18	1870
James Watt (Philosopher)	19	1736
Gen. Robert E. Lee (Confederate Gen.)	19	1807
Edgar Allen Poe (Poet and Essayist)	19	1809
George Trumbill Ladd	19	1842

AQUARIUS—January 21 to February 19.

By those who in this sign are born,
No gems save Chrysolite should be worn;
They will insure your constancy,
True friendship and fidelity.

	Date	Year
John Charles Fremont (Pathfinder)............	21	1813
King Oscar II. (King of Sweden)..............	21	1829
Stonewall Jackson (Gen. in Confederate Army)..	21	1824
Henry VIII. (King of England)...............	22	1547
Sir Francis Bacon (Philosopher and Essayist).....	22	1561
Lord Byron (English Poet)..................	22	1788
Coquelin (French Actor)....................	23	1841
Joseph H. Choate (Lawyer, Minister to England).	24	1832
Charles Fox..............................	24	1749
Robert Burns (Scottish Poet)................	25	1759
Cornelius N. Bliss (Banker)..................	26	1833
Ernest Henrich Weber.......................	26	1795
Mozart (Composer).........................	27	1756
John C. Black (Federal General)..............	27	1839
Samuel Gompers (Chief of Labor Union)........	27	1850
James Ward	27	1843
Henry M. Stanley, Sir (African Explorer)......	28	1841
Lyman J. Gage (Banker).....................	28	1836
Thomas Paine	29	1737
Wm. McKinley (Pres. U. S.).................	29	1843
Emanuel Swedenborg (Spiritual Seer and Writer).	29	1688
James G. Blaine (Statesman and Politician)......	31	1830
Abner Rush (Inspirational Writer).............	1	1832
G. Stanley Hall............................	1	1846
Lord Salisbury (Prime Minister of England)....	3	1830
Dwight L. Moody (Evangelist)...............	5	1837
Hiram S. Maxim (Inventor of Rapid Firing Gun)	5	1840
Sir Henry Irving (English Tragedian)..........	6	1838
William M. Evarts (Lawyer and Statesman).....	6	1818
Prof. C. Lloyd Morgan (Educator)...........	6	1852
Aaron Burr (Statesman U. P., U. S. under Jefferson)	6	1856
Rev. Samuel Wakefield (Famous Methodist)....	6	1799
Charles Dickens (Author)....................	7	1812
Richard Watson Gilder (Editor Century Mag.)..	8	1844
Jules Verne ("Around the World in 80 Days")..	8	1828
John Ruskin (Philosopher and Writer)..........	8	1819
Samuel J. Tilden (Lawyer and Politician).......	9	1814
George Ade (Author and Writer)..............	9	1866
Hon. Daniel S. Lamont (Lawyer and Politician)..	9	1851

Charles Lamb (English Essayist and Critic)	10	1775
Chief Justice M. W. Fuller (Supreme Court)	11	1833
Thomas A. Edison (Inventor)	11	1847
Lord Brassey (English Traveler and Writer)	11	1836
Charles Darwin (Evolutionist, Author, Scientist)	12	1809
Abraham Lincoln (Pres. U. S.)	12	1809
F. E. Ormsby (Pyramid and Cube University)	12	——
Talleyrand (French Diplomatist)	13	1754
Cyrus Wakefield (Philanthropist)	14	1811
Cazotte (Astrologer)	15	1421
Madame Marcella Sembrich (Opera Singer)	15	1858
Susan B. Anthony (Reformer, Lecturer)	15	1820
Cyrus H. McCormick (Manufacturer of Reapers)	15	1809
Galileo (Astronomer)	15	1564
George Kennan (Traveler, Journalist and Author)	16	1845
George Ernst Haeckel (German Scientist)	16	1834
Li Hung Chang (Grand Man of China)	16	1823
Wilson Barrett (Actor)	18	1846
Dr. Ernest Mach (German Scientist and Writer)	18	1838
Adelina Patti (Singer)	19	1843
Nicholas Copemicus (Found. Mod. Astronomy)	19	1473

PISCES—February 19 to March 21.
The Pisces born will find
Sincerity and peace of mind—
Freedom from passion and from care,
If they the Blue Sapphire will wear.

	Date	Year
Voltaire (Prolific Writer and Foe to Shame)	20	1694
Joseph Jefferson (Actor)	20	1829
Cardinal Newman (R. C. Churchman—English)	21	1801
James Russell Lowell (Poet)	22	1819
George Washington (Pres. U. S.)	22	1732
Bishop John H. Vincent (M. E. Church)	23	1832
John Habberton (Author "Helen's Babies." Journalist)	24	1842
Camille Flammarion (Astronomer)	25	1842
Joseph Le Conte (Philosopher, Writer)	26	1823
Wm. F. Cody (Buffalo Bill)	26	1846
Victor Hugo (French Author and Patriot)	26	1802
H. W. Longfellow (Poet)	27	1848

Ellen Terry (English Actress)	27	1848
Wm. Dean Howells (Author-Poet)	1	1837
Augustus St. Gaudens (Sculptor)	1	1848
Chopin (Composer)	1	1809
Stephen Ohin (Liberal Methodist)	2	1791
Carl Schurz (Publicist and Mugwump)	2	1829
Wm. B. Allison (Senator, Politician and Lawyer)	2	1829
Pope Leo XIII. (Oldest Pope in Service)	2	1810
Geo. M. Pullman (Capitalist and Manufacturer)	3	1831
Alexander Graham Bell (Telephone Inventor)	3	1847
Seneca D. Kimbark (Merchant of Chicago)	4	1832
Gen. Philip H. Sheridan (Federal General)	6	1831
Elizabeth Barrett Browning (Author)	6	1809
Edwin H. Conger (Minister to China, Boxer War)	7	1843
Rufus Blanchard (Pioneer Map Maker)	7	1821
Americus Vespucius (Explorer. America named for him)	9	1451
Arthur Pue Gorman (Politician, Lawyer)	11	1839
Lillie Langtry (Actress and Beauty)	12	1852
Geo. Berkley (English Metaphysician)	12	1685
Andrew Jackson (Pres. U. S.)	15	1767
James Madison (Pres. U. S.)	16	1751
Dr. Ephraim Epstein (Ed. Alkaloidal Mag., Phila.)	17	——
Princess Louise (Wife of Edward VII of England)	18	1848
Grover Cleveland (Pres. U. S.)	18	1837
William Penn Nixon (Editor-Journalist)	19	1833
William Jennings Bryan (Candidate for Pres. 2)	19	1860
Johann Paul Frederick Richter (Huromist)	21	1763
Johann Sebastian Bach (Composer)	21	1685

www.ingramcontent.com/pod-product-compliance
Lightning Source LLC
Chambersburg PA
CBHW030342310726
48979CB00001B/144

9781434496102